Michelle woke coated in sweat, shivering as the February cold hit her wet skin. She ran her fingers through her long hair, pushing it back from her perspiration-covered forehead. How could she be hot and cold at the same time? Only a few seconds and the nightmare dissipated. Once or twice a month, Mitch returned in her dreams. The worse ones were when she killed him and he wasn't a zombie. She shuddered, wrapping the covers around her body.

She counted to twenty with deep breaths in and deep breaths out. Her familiar mantra of 'It's only a dream' echoed in her head. Her heart rate slowed and her shoulders slumped in relief. The dregs of sleep disappeared with the shouts of children outside her motor home. A thump hit the door as someone tagged safe. A smile crossed her face and the world seemed a little better, as strange as that was. When the world went to hell, even small things could make it possible to get through the day.

Other books by Jill James

The Lake Willowbee Series
Divorce, Interrupted
Dare To Trust
Defend My Love
The Reluctant Bride
Waking Up For Christmas
Baby Steps and Snowflakes

Shifters of San Laura Series
Dangerous Shift

Time of Zombies Series
Love in the Time of Zombies
The Zombie Hunter's Wife
A Time to Kill Zombies

Short Stories
The Christmas Con
Rogue Vantage

THE
ZOMBIE
HUNTER'S
WIFE

JILL JAMES

 Gray Sweater Press

The Zombie Hunter's Wife
Time of Zombies, Book 2
All Rights Reserved.
Copyright 2015 Jill James
ISBN# 978-0692554401
Cover Art © Elaina Lee at For The Muse Designs
All rights reserved – Used with permission

Gray Sweater Press
www.graysweaterpress.com

DEDICATION

Thanks to RJ Kennett for showing me zombie books could be fun to write.

Thank you to Charity Truth Wilson who gave Rogue Vantage their name via a Facebook contest.

As always, thank you to my family for knowing I need writing time. You are the best.

CHAPTER ONE

Anger and fear battled for territory within her as her husband walked up the hill to their home. Even if he hadn't still been in his dark-blue SFPD uniform, Michelle Greggs would recognize Mitch anywhere. The half of his face she could see retained the stunning good looks she'd fallen for all those years ago when they were in high school, when he'd been captain of the football team and she'd been the nerdy girl who beat out the head cheerleader to win his heart. He turned slightly, his head set at a tilted angle and his neck twisted as if broken. The other half of his face was in ravaged ruins, his eyeball pulled from the socket, hung by a tendon, and rested on his bloody and torn cheek. Black mucous oozed from his wide-open mouth and ran down his police uniform shirt to mix with the blood dripping from his chin, making the dark shirt glisten sickly in the sunshine. The shirt she'd ironed with loving care last night was encrusted with thick gore. The pants with their knife-sharp military pleats were torn and bloody as well.

Her breath caught on a wheezing gasp. His head turned and one blue eye tracked her as she skittered backward, reaching, grabbing for the doorknob.

From two houses away he'd heard her small inhalation of breath.

From two houses away she heard his ravenous moan, the sound rising as he spotted fresh meat.

She bit her lip and stifled her screams as he moved faster. The thing that had been her soul mate shambled closer, tripping over the crack in the sidewalk. The one he kept telling her he would fix and now he never would.

A deeper, trailing moan rumbled from his chest and the hair rose on the nape of her neck. *How had he gotten so close, so fast?* She forced her mind to concentrate. His hands came up and reached for her. The nails dirty and broken, filled with unmentionable crud, traveled across her gaze.

Her heart raced and thumped in her chest. She couldn't breathe. Maybe if she stood perfectly still he would leave. Her cry broke the silence as Mitch stumbled into her and his hands encircled her throat. She brought her arms up and pushed against his filthy, slippery shirt, but the hands tightened as his moans grew and he pulled her toward his chomping jaw filled with sharp, broken teeth tainted with flesh and blood.

Blackness took the edge of her vision and she stopped pushing. His fetid breath whooshed over her and she gagged. If she just let it happen, they would be together forever. They had no children. No one to leave behind, the flu took care of that. How hard could dying be?

I don't want to die.

The thought, along with a million others raced through her in a millisecond and added steel to her spine. With force, she brought the heel of her shoe to his shin and kicked as hard as she could, just as he'd taught her. His moans stopped like a broken wind-up toy as he toppled sideways and fell to the ground, his leg bent impossibly backward. He lay there like a helpless turtle trying to turn over, his athletic prowess gone.

Before he could get his hands around to push up, Michelle reached for his gun on the service belt. She unsnapped the holster, pulled Mitch's service weapon out, and pointed it at her husband's face.

No. Not her husband. This thing was not her husband. This undead thing stole her husband from her.

Her vision blurred with tears. They froze on her wind-chilled cheeks as they poured, hot then cold, down her face. She put her foot on his chest, shoved the gun into the hole where his eye should be, and pulled the trigger.

Her rubbery legs gave out and she fell to the cement steps as the echo of the gunshot buzzed in her head. Her hand shook until the gun left her grip and clattered to the pavement. She stared at the thing that had been Mitch just a few hours ago.

"You promised to come back," she whispered at him.

"You promised to come back," she screamed at him.

Her yell echoed down the deserted street, her only answer the cry of a seagull winging overhead. Her neighbors had left days ago. Mitch and Michelle's house the only occupied one on the block. The army had promised one final sweep before dusk. She'd begged Mitch to just leave. He'd refused to go AWOL from the SFPD. He'd promised to go in this morning and tell them he was leaving.

Four hours.

Four hours and her husband was dead, and then undead, and now truly dead.

And she was alone.

So fast. Everything had happened so damned fast. Just months since billions died worldwide from the flu. Just weeks since the president of the United States ordered a vaccine put in the food and water. Just days since the dead didn't stay dead. Just days since they'd infected others with their blood and their bites.

Sounds intruded into her solitude. The moans of the undead echoed in the distance, lost to the earthshaking booms further to the south as the army destroyed entire blocks of apartments and homes to seal off the city. The last news report on the television this morning before it went to snowy static said they would destroy the Caldecott Tunnel as well.

She shuddered, her hands shaking as she picked up the gun and set it on her lap. She'd spent her whole life in San Francisco and it wasn't home anymore, now it would be the city of the undead. No more views of the bay. No more drives over the Golden Gate Bridge to Marin for shopping and exploring antiques shops. No more.

"Damn you." Her yell bounced off the houses. She shook her head. She didn't even know who she was damning, God, the zombies, or herself for killing the only man she had ever loved.

A Humvee rumbled up her street and a soldier in dusty, bloody camo jumped out.

"Ready to go?"

"Just a minute, please," she begged over her shoulder as she laid Mitch out straight and placed his hands on his chest. Falling to her knees, she kissed the undamaged cheek. A sob caught and broke loose.

"Come on, lady. If we don't get to the evac site on schedule, they blow the bridge without us."

She hefted the duffel bag onto her shoulder, all of her old life contained in the one bag the army was allowing. Mitch's bag sat abandoned on the steps. She turned away and walked down the sidewalk. The soldier stopped her at the vehicle's door.

"No weapons."

"It's my husband's service revolver. I don't want to lose it," Michelle pleaded, glancing back.

"The drivers are collecting weapons. You'll get them returned when you get to where you are going."

"Thank you. Where would that be?" She forced her mind to move forward, because there was sure as hell no going back.

She climbed in the rear and the soldier got in the front passenger seat. "The last group out is going to Brentwood. In the far East Bay. I've heard it's nice. Farm country. Little town. Whole hella lot less zombs."

Leaning back, Michelle closed her eyes. She'd been to Brentwood as a kid with her parents during cherry-picking season. The town could be quaint, but it wasn't San Francisco. As a little girl she'd dreamed of traveling the world, but no city in the world compared to the city by the bay.

"Ma'am, you got anymore family we can pick up? Got a few seats left if we hurry."

She opened her eyes to look at a man who looked too young to shave, let alone be in the army. "My parents died during the influenza pandemic and that cop back there was my husband. I don't have a family.

"What about you? Where are you from?" she whispered.

The man swallowed deeply and his Adam's apple bobbed, while a devastated look came over him. "I'm from New York City. I don't know."

News and information from outside the state had ended almost as soon as the dead rose. The last info from New York City mentioned nukes.

She wasn't old enough to be this boy's mother, but she felt like it after the last few months. Things spiraled from bad to worse to—to this.

Reaching out, she put her hand on his shoulder. "I'm sorry."

At a loss for any other words of comfort she pulled back and closed her eyes again until they stopped and the sound of people talking and moving around outside the vehicle intruded on the silent shell she'd erected during the drive. The roar of engines came and went. Men yelled and children cried.

Grabbing her duffel bag and getting out of the Humvee, she was soon pushed and prodded into a line of people headed to a fortified school bus. Desperation peeled off the people along with body odor. The breeze off the bay carried it across the parking lot. Sheets of battered metal covered the windows with a few slits left open for air. She shivered. Such a small barrier to keep out the abominations rambling across the city.

A young woman with long black hair stepped onto the bus in front of her. Stepping forward, she replied to the questions from the clipboard-holding police officer. Even with his nameplate she didn't recognize his name or face.

"Name?"

"Mrs. Michelle Greggs."

"Mr. Greggs?"

She shook her head and wiped a tear running down her face.

"Dead or undead?"

"Dead," she whispered.

"Confirmed?"

"Yes, I shot him in the head," she spit out between a clenched jaw.

"Thank you. Next."

She tripped up the stairs, shaking her head at the pit their world had fallen into. A place where shooting your husband was the right thing to do. How had chaos taken hold so fast? A hand grasped her elbow and caught her before she fell.

"You dropped your bag."

Turning to get it, she fell backward on her butt as the police officer at the door managed to push her inside as he was pulled to the ground by a horde of zombies. Blood splattered the glass and stair treads before the driver shut the doors. The sheets of metal hid the carnage, but not the screams for help or the moans of undead hunger.

Again a hand reached for her elbow and helped her up. She looked into the face of the woman with long, dark hair who had been in front of her.

"I see an empty seat near the back," the woman said as the bus started moving.

The two of them grabbed handholds to walk to the rear as the bus bucked and swayed, rolling over bumps that had been people. She started crying again as she fell into the seat and the woman fell in beside her.

Wiping her tears, Michelle stared at the woman beside her. She had on a suit that probably cost more than Mitch made in a month, heels, and pantyhose. Who wore pantyhose anymore? Probably women who wore luminous pearls around their neck and diamond studs in their ears that looked to be a few carats apiece.

She glanced around but everyone seemed occupied with the people near them. This woman looked as if she were all alone too. "Thank you for helping me there. I'm Michelle Greggs."

The woman shook her hand. "Emily Gray. Are you alone?"

She shuddered and nodded. The anguish was all too fresh to go there. She tried to change the subject. "And you?"

"Yes," Emily said as she reached and removed her necklace and put it in a clutch purse she held. Next, went the earrings. She pulled a silver necklace out of her shirt and placed it on the fabric.

Her fingers played with the pendant as she talked. "My mother and father died a couple of days ago, trying to get to me. My in-laws died of the flu epidemic. My husband died a couple of weeks ago."

Her voice was gruff. Definitely something there. "Did you have to kill him?"

A twisted smile came across her face. "Oh, no. That was the police. Him and the hooker in the motel. His screams alerted the other customers and they called for help." The announcement was made so calmly they could have been chatting over tea and scones.

Her mouth fell open. Emily reached and patted her hand. "It's okay, dear. It wasn't the first time, but it definitely was the last."

The bus slowed and stopped at an intersection. The pounding of meaty fists hit the sides of the bus. Bloody, gore-covered fingers pushed through the slits, slivers of bone poking through skin. Screams echoed inside the bus, overriding the moans outside. Women hugged men and children grasped at their parents, their little hands holding on with all their strength.

"I killed him," she got out between sobs, not sure if they were for sadness or fright. "He was the moon, the sun, and the stars to me and I had to kill him. He promised to come home and we would leave. He came back to our home as the undead and he made me kill him. How could he do that to me?"

A hand patted her back and rubbed in comforting circles. "There, there. Maybe some small sense of him was left and he knew he had to get home."

"I don't want to talk about it ever again. I don't want to think about it ever again."

She just wanted to find four solid walls and a roof and safety. Michelle wrapped her arms around herself and prayed for the security the insanity had ripped away. Like a mantra for serenity, she whispered repeatedly the name of the little town at the end of this ghastly ride.

"Brentwood."

CHAPTER TWO

Rule #1   *Wash work clothes every day. Blood and brain matter are impossible to remove if you let them set.*

One year later
Oakley, California
RV Storage yard, R-1 base

Michelle woke coated in sweat, shivering as the February cold hit her wet skin. She ran her fingers through her long hair, pushing it back from her perspiration-covered forehead. How could she be hot and cold at the same time? Only a few seconds and the nightmare dissipated. Once or twice a month, Mitch returned in her dreams. The worse ones were when she killed him and he wasn't a zombie. She shuddered, wrapping the covers around her body.

She counted to twenty with deep breaths in and deep breaths out. Her familiar mantra of 'It's only a dream' echoed in her head. Her heart rate slowed and her shoulders slumped in relief. The dregs of sleep disappeared with the shouts of children outside her motor home. A thump hit the door as someone tagged safe. A smile crossed her face and the world seemed a little better, as strange as that was. When the world went to hell, even small things could make it possible to get through the day.

Jumping out of the covers, she dressed in layers, making it easier to peel off extra ones later in the day as the weather warmed up. She was used to layers from living in San Francisco her whole life, but not used to the warmth of a February afternoon in the East Bay.

She'd spent last February here, but it still amazed her that winter could be so unwinter-like, with some days as warm as summer in the city.

She sighed, missing the fog and the ocean breeze off the bay. Pulling her hair back into a ponytail, she flung open the door to sunshine and a wind that already carried a hint of the almost-balmy warmth they would face in the afternoon, as if spring was right around the corner.

Her boys raced to her side. Yelling and pushing at each other to be the first. The two oldest pushed each other, knocking over the middle one in the process. The littlest boy reached her first today. Dylan's small body rocketed into her, knocking her off balance. Her arms swept around him and gave the little one a giant hug. Two seconds later she was hit with three more boys as the oldest, Aiden and Bryant hugged her together and Connor squeezed in, as usual.

"How are my RVers today?"

"Mom," echoed in four different voices with the exasperation exactly the same. It still thrilled her to be called mom by her adopted sons.

"That is so lame," Aiden added, being the spokesman for the group as the oldest and a born leader. "We aren't RVers. We are Rogue Vantage."

She bit her lip to stop a laugh from escaping. Four serious faces stared at her. Michelle reached out and ruffled little Dylan's hair. "Sorry. How is the Rogue Vantage doing today?"

Smiles broke out across white, tan, and brown faces. Her friend, Emily was always sprouting off that the zombie apocalypse allowed everyone to start anew. She could play along if her boys wanted to sound like a 'gang.' Although, with the oldest being ten years old and the youngest just turned six, they weren't too tough of a gang. Her breath still caught in her throat at the memory of these four kids being the only ones left at this RV storage facility after a deadly virus took all the adults and everyone else just left. Her eyes watered with the thought of the children living with dead bodies too heavy for their young arms to move and dispose of properly.

She cheered up as they pulled her toward the eating area of the compound with shouts of *breakfast* and *food* and *now*. Today, Dylan stayed by her side as the other three rushed to get a place in line. Over their heads she could see Beth Evans and Miranda Stevens had food duty today. Her gaze traveled over Beth's pregnant stomach as the girls moved back and forth to serve the group. The stomach seemed to have ballooned overnight. Last month Beth had started borrowing bigger clothes from some of the ladies and now she looked like the scavengers would need to find a maternity store for her.

Someone bumped into her from behind and she knew without looking that it was her friend, Emily. She'd know that stomach anywhere. If there was anyone bigger than Beth at the moment, it was her friend who was at least a month behind the young girl in her pregnancy.

Turning, she looked down. Even knowing what to expect she still gasped. "You look like you're going to give birth any day."

"Thanks a lot," Emily said, lightly smacking her arm. "I still have months to go."

"No way," Dylan put in. "You'll explode by then." He spread his arms and made the sound of an explosion.

Michelle held her breath as Emily's eyes watered up and she started crying. "Oh, sure. Pick on the fat lady."

"Crying? There's no crying in the zombie apocalypse. Zombie hunters don't cry," she said, hoping to turn the unusual mood around.

Emily started laughing and crying at the same time and Michelle let out her held breath. "Maybe you'll have the first triplets or quads of the apocalypse."

"Bite your tongue," her friend said. "No fucking way."

"Yeah, no fucking way," Dylan parroted.

At first she'd been appalled by the boys' behavior and language but she'd learned quickly if she 'mothered' too much she'd lose them. They were the first generation of AZ, after the Z virus. Somehow, worrying about cussing and minor scuffles seemed ridiculous when you had bigger problems to worry about, like being some zombie's lunch or how to have enough food for dinner.

Laughing, they all got their meals and moved to a picnic table. Dylan stayed by her side and Emily sat across from them. The rest of the boys scattered to eat with friends. She looked around and sighed.

"I never would have thought I'd miss The Streets of Brentwood mall so much."

Emily stuffed food in her mouth, swallowed, and looked around. "Pretty bad, when eating at a burger place with folding chairs and tables, seems like eating at Top of the Mark in comparison."

She wouldn't know anything about Top of the Mark, San Francisco's premier restaurant. It would have been beyond Mitch's paycheck to go there without some serious dollar stretching . . . for months. Michelle stared at the gray cinderblocks making up the walls of their haven and sighed. "I just miss being able to see for miles around. All I see all day long is motor homes and gray walls."

"You could go outside, you know," Emily threw out there with an evil twinkle in her eye.

"Not me. No way. You zombie hunters can go risk your lives. The ride here was scary enough after we blew up the old compound. Maybe I'll paint some hills and trees on the walls. That's as close to 'outside' as I'm getting."

"Chicken," Emily said.

"Bawk, bawk," Dylan added.

"Traitor," she murmured, pulling him in close to her with an arm wrapped around his shoulders.

"Need I remind you, you jumped off that fence and ran outside fast enough when I got here," Emily said.

She shuddered. "I thought you were dead. That's different. If I had been thinking clearly, I wouldn't have done it at all."

"Maybe you were thinking clearly for once," Emily mumbled.

"Mr. Teddy. Mr. Teddy," several young voices called out.

She turned around in her seat to see Teddy Ridgewood and several other men returning from zombie hunting and killing for the morning shift. As usual, the enormous, African-American man was covered from shaved head to boots in blood and gore. Sighing, she got up from the table. As if blood and gore could disguise broad shoulders, flat abs, and a face that got her libido going in seconds flat. She swallowed and looked away. She wasn't going there—ever again. Even if Teddy was a dark chocolate mountain of yumminess. Sex appeal and lust meant nothing when a man put duty before you. For him, it wasn't even duty. The man acted like hunting zombies was a video game with infinite lives. She shook her head. Nope, one and dead. Or undead, and then dead. A knot grew in her throat. Never again, she vowed silently.

"Laundry duty sucks sometimes," she mumbled to Emily.

"You could wait until they're all undressed," her friend said.

She stared at the other woman. "No way. Do you know how hard blood and guts is to get out if I wait for them to finally change clothes, and to remember to bring the dirty ones to me? Impossible, that's what." She turned to walk away.

"By all means, go strip Teddy out of his clothes," Emily said, with what sounded suspiciously like a laugh covered by a fake cough.

Her face heated up to flame temperature. "I have to get *all* the clothes."

"Of course you do. I see you rushing to get Morales' too," Emily yelled in a sarcastic tone as Michelle stomped off. Sometimes it sucked to have a friend who could read her so well. She needed to work on her poker face.

* * *

Teddy Ridgewood sat on the wooden bench, trying to pry off his gore-covered boots.

"Damn it," he muttered as he pushed one boot with the foot of the other. He couldn't afford to lose another pair. His size fourteen boots were darned near impossible to find. He'd been in sneakers for weeks until they'd found this pair at a workman's clothing store.

Looking up, he spotted Michelle Greggs. The woman was a firecracker for sure, always yelling at him for his dirty clothes. As if she thought they could kill the skinbags all day and come home looking as clean as if they'd been to the office, writing reports or something.

He tried to be extra nice to her, but something about him always set her off. He smiled every time he saw her. He talked to her quiet-like, knowing his big booming voice startled some women. He spent time with her boys, which was no biggie. The little ones tugged at his heart, making it ache at the thought of them here all alone for months. A chill went up his spine at the thought of the world they were inheriting.

But the woman didn't crack a smile at him. Although, he did catch her staring at him at odd times. He would glance back and she would whip her head around fast enough to wrench her neck something awful.

"Mr. Ridgewood," she announced as she approached. Her hips swayed in a feminine way that made his hands itch to explore, even with her 'don't touch' airs. Her face could have graced the Madonna as a statue in a chapel. Her voice was sweet, when it wasn't yelling at him. Sometimes he sat out of view just to hear her talk to her boys with those soft, dulcet tones.

She snapped on Latex gloves and he jumped in his seat. Miss Emily had explained that they were an idiosyncrasy,as if they all weren't already infected, but they made him feel dirtier than the blood, guts, and gore alone. Her gaze raked over him and heat covered his face. He lowered his head even though the red wouldn't show on his dark cheeks.

"Sorry, Mrs. Greggs. I know you got things to do. Seem to be having trouble with my boots."

Michelle squatted down and started untying the laces.

It shouldn't have been erotic in the least, having his shoes taken off like he was a child, but tell that to the erection straining against the zipper of his pants. He stared at her glossy dark hair, pulled back into a ponytail he'd like to let loose and run his fingers through, and he imagined her all too easily in this position, and not for untying his shoes.

She stood and he realized his boots were off. The woman turned her back and held out her hand. "I need the rest of your clothes. I'll try to save your boots, but I can't make any promises."

Peeling off his clothes, Teddy wondered, not for the first time, what she thought when she looked at him. Even if she hadn't been such a petite woman, he would still have been large next to her. Even with his boots off, he didn't believe she would reach much farther than his chest with the top of her head.

He'd never considered himself an overly modest man, but his time of being alone as the self-proclaimed King of Pittsburg had changed him. Being alone was a lot easier than being surrounded by people all day long in the small confines of the RV facility. Standing near Michelle and stripping was nerve-racking as well. He needed the time away from the yard each day before it started feeling like a prison.

At last, he was down to his boxer briefs, which he was able to leave on. Teddy grabbed a towel from the bench and wrapped it as far as it would go around his ample waist. He shot a quick glance to reassure himself that the erection was hidden. He pressed it down. Good enough.

Michelle turned around to stare him in the face and it returned to full attention. At least her glance seemed to stay on his face, at least most of the time. That glance did seem to wander to his chest a few times. Her cheeks were red and she seemed to search for words.

"I—I'll have these ready by dinner." She bent and picked up his boots. "These may take longer to dry."

"I can clean them." He reached for the boots and caught her hand instead. She pulled back so fast the clothes fell to the ground. They both reached for them, but she yanked them away.

Standing, he stepped back. "Thank you, Mrs. Greggs."

"No problem, umm—umm Mr. Ridgewood."

She strolled back to the laundry area, holding his boots in one hand and his clothes in the other with her arms straight out, as if they were contaminated with more than zombie guts.

Teddy shook his head and walked across the cracked asphalt to his motor home. He laughed and felt a smile break on his face. Just because it was the zombie apocalypse didn't mean men had any better hope of understanding women than before the world went to hell in a hand basket, as his mother used to say. But he sure wanted to understand Michelle Greggs. Because for just a second there she'd looked at him as a man, a man she liked looking at, not as a nuisance.

A shower and a set of clean clothes later and he was ready to find his friend, Seth Ripley to see if he understood women any better than Teddy did.

CHAPTER THREE

The Fruitful Harvest Church
Highway 4, between Antioch and Oakley

Canvas snapped in the constant wind. The moans of the Resurrected carried from the cages on the edge of the encampment. The tent filled with cries of the captured women before a few well-placed slaps from the men surrounding them brought silence.

Billy Joe Bennett slid his leg down from the arm of the chair. Sitting up straight, he turned to the woman beside him.

"Is this all, Roberta?"

She nodded. "Yes, Reverend. A heavy march of the Resurrected has been through here. The men found this group in a broken-down car up the highway."He pushed off from the chair and marched to the sniveling group on their knees in the middle of the tent. Two men stood guard at the flapping entrance. The three young women were one of each—a blonde, a brunette, and a redhead. The fourth female had salt and pepper strands of hair covering her head and face in a tangled mess.

Reaching down, he grabbed the blonde's chin and yanked her head up. Dark-blue eyes were the best feature in a plain face. His hand dropped away and he moved on. The brunette had promise, if her waist-length curls were any indication. He leaned down and grasped a silky handful. She moaned as he pulled her head back. The face of an angel glared back at him with the devil in her eyes. Good. He liked them with spunk. It made it so much fun to beat it out of them. He hated red hair, even his own, so he walked right past the last young woman huddled in a ball on the ground.

He placed himself in front of the last female. Shaking hands reached up and pushed the gray-speckled dark hair out of her face. A face that had lived a long lifetime with the lines and wrinkles to prove it stared back at him. The gentle face of a grandmother or beloved aunt.

"If you're going to kill me, do it already," she cried out.

Billy Joe took her hand and pulled her up. "I can't kill you, for you have not sinned against me, old woman. I can only give you resurrection."

"I don't understand . . . " she managed to get out as he pulled his knife, yanked her in close, and stabbed her in the chest.

The body fell to the ground, twitched a few times, and went still, her eyes glazing over in death. A hush filled the tent until a moment later she rolled over and rose with moans and a snapping of her jaw.

Cries of 'hallelujah' rang out from his group, along with the screams of the captured females sitting by the newly-risen as he wiped the blade on his pants.

Two of his men rushed over and restrained the woman, tying her hands behind her back and with some difficulty getting a gag into her mouth. They dragged her out of the tent as the younger women settled down into hysterical whimpers.

He grew light-headed as the blood rushed to his racing heart. The power of life, death, and resurrection had been placed in his hands by God. Only he could decide which was granted.

With a spreading of his arms, the women were grabbed and yanked to their feet. A glare at them and silence reigned again in his canvas cathedral. He turned and walked back to his chair, sitting and leaning against the high back, like a king on his throne. Bubbling laughter escaped him.

Pushing down the glee, he grew serious and turned his gaze on the sniveling females. It just reiterated his belief in the faults of the weaker sex. Females needed men to be in control. The world had been going in the wrong direction for too long. The influenza pandemic and the virus that raised the dead just reset the world, back to where it belonged.

"God sent a plague upon us. He wanted to cleanse the Earth of its evil. This church, Fruitful Harvest, is the new beginning. A return to the ways of our forefathers. A return to the right way. A return to man as the master and woman as the obedient servant, the bearer of his children, the submissive sitting at his feet, waiting to provide his every wish."

He pointed to each of the young women. "You will each be chosen as a bride of the church, a bride of man, or one of the anointed Resurrected. I alone have this power. God has given me the right to choose your future path."

Pushing away from the chair, he walked toward them. Their tears increased, music to his ears. He had been given the power of life and undeath. He stepped in front of the redhead. Grabbing her chin, he forced her to look at him.

"What is your name, woman?"

She glared at him and refused to speak.

In a split-second the knife was under her chin, piercing the skin, a bead of red running down the blade. "I will ask one more time, and then you will be joining the Resurrected. What is your name?"

Her throat convulsed as she swallowed. "April."

His hand dropped and he slid the knife into the sheath on his belt. "See, that wasn't so hard, was it? I'm sure this next question won't be either. Are you a virgin? Think before you answer. If you lie, you will not be resurrected, you'll just be dead as your lies will be a sin against me."

The young woman's face turned beet red, bright enough to match her hair. Her 'yes' was low, but he didn't need it, her blush had proclaimed it loud and clear.

"Elias," he called to a large, ugly man standing to his left. "I believe you are in need of a wife as Abigail proved infertile and joined the Resurrected ones. April is yours. Claim her and mark her as your wife and helpmate."

The girl tried to pull away, but her meager strength was no match for the two men, the one holding her and the other now at her side. One held her wrists in his large hands as the man named Elias stepped up behind her and grabbed a handful of her long auburn hair.

The man pulled his knife from his belt and turned to the group. "I claim April as my wife and helpmate. I mark her with her shorn hair to show her fidelity and loyalty as a good wife." The knife slid through her hair with ease and the man dropped handfuls to the ground.

Billy Joe grasped his hands in front of this mouth to hide his smirk. *Good riddance. Her shining, copper-tinted hair was too much of a reminder of his whore-mother. Her glossy hair, red-painted lips, and skintight outfits as she strutted across the stage of his father's steel and glass cathedral.*

He pulled himself back to the present as Elias finished and the young woman was left with ragged and uneven tufts of hair, the luxurious tresses in a pile at her feet. Her whimpering cries filled the tent, but were soon drowned out from the ringing 'amens' from the church members.

Walking up to Elias, he placed his hand on the man's shoulder. "Go with God and may you find your wife submissive and pure."

"Go with God and may you find your wife submissive and pure," echoed the congregation.

The large man grabbed the young woman by the arm and dragged her from the tent, her squeals and struggles ignored by the group.

Once they were outside the flap and the girl's cries died away, Billy Joe moved on. He strolled to the blonde. It wasn't that she was ugly; she was just what his daddy would have said, 'was rode hard and put away wet.'

"What is your name?"

"Teri."

"Are you a virgin?"

"Yeah, like five or six years ago," she said, and then spit in his face.

He backhanded her and smiled as she hit the ground. Nodding to a young man, he grabbed a handful of greasy hair and pulled her to her knees. One of his men came over and pulled her arms behind her back. Billy Joe held on to her hair and

28

stretched her neck. A simple nod and the young man lifted his ax and brought it down on Teri's neck. He jumped back as the blood spurted from her decapitation across the canvas floor.

He raised her head with his hand still wrapped tight in her hair. "This is the face of evil. Don't forget it. Woman was made to be pure, wedded, or dead; there is no other state of her being. Her purity belongs to God until a husband claims her."

Dropping the head like a piece of garbage he was done with, he moved to the last young woman. She stared straight ahead, her eyes glazed and shocked.

"What is your name?"

"Maya," she stuttered out.

"Are you a virgin?"

She nodded her head.

He glanced at the body and head a few men were removing. "You see the penalty for lying, don't you?"

Her head came up and she glanced in his eyes. "Yes, I'm a virgin," she spoke loud and clear.

He grabbed a handful of long, dark curls and pulled her to his side. He pushed on her until her knees hit the ground and he held her there at his feet.

"I've heard the word of God and he has told me that Maya is to be a bride of God, to be my bride. I am to mold her and make her into a shining example of what it is to be a wife and helpmate."

His now-first wife, Roberta, came to his side and placed a hand on his shoulder. "Go with God and may you find your wife submissive and pure."

The congregation repeated the benediction. No one but Billy Joe felt Roberta's nails digging into his shoulder, which was the only reason she still had a hand to be squeezing his shoulder with.

He smiled as the congregation congratulated him. *There was more than one way to punish and torment an unruly first wife. Like making her watch as he deflowered wife number two.*

CHAPTER FOUR

Rule #2 *Don't baby the children; they have to grow up to be zombie-hunters, even if you don't want them to be anything but children. That time is past.*

RV Storage yard
Oakley, California

Michelle gripped her hands together and pressed her lips hard. She would not embarrass Dylan again by demanding the men not teach him to shoot and stab the skinbags. No, not the men. Teddy. The giant man was down on one knee behind the little boy, holding on to his thin arms as he fired a gun.

She jumped again as the gun fired and the sound carried from the practice field to where she stood atop the wall. The shooting range had never made her jump when she was the one doing the firing. But there seemed something wrong with teaching a six-year old to shoot for survival.

Her gaze had been so intent on the boy and the strong man at this back that she would have missed the stumbling zombie headed their way, tripping over the sun-baked dirt, if not for the gasp in her ear.

Her mouth moved but no words tumbled out. No scream of a warning. She stared in horror as Emily reached over her shoulder for the ever-present crossbow she no longer carried. Footsteps thundered down the boards of the scaffolding as Emily's husband, Seth joined them. He pulled a gun out of the holster on his belt, his finger tightened on the trigger, and then nothing.

He couldn't take the shot with Dylan and Teddy in the way, she could see that. Emily yelled down to the man, "Teddy, your two o'clock." Her fingernails dug into her palms as the man's head swiveled to spot the zomb' just feet from his position. In a move that was almost too quick to follow, he grabbed Dylan to his chest and raised his foot to hit the undead in the stomach and pushed him away.

Before anyone could do anything else, Dylan raised the gun still in his hands and shot the skinbag in the head. The zomb' dropped at their feet.

Her mouth dropped open as Dylan and Teddy high-fived each other with great big grins on their faces. Her hand itched to smack them both. Didn't they get it? Zombies weren't supposed to be able to get this close. The repel sound Jed Long ran twenty-four hours a day through the mounted speakers was supposed to keep them away—far away. God knows it was supposed to do something useful for all the aching teeth and headaches they had to put up with to endure the ultrasonic hum all the time.

Seth hugged Emily and gave her a quick kiss before he scrambled down the ladder and she assumed out the gate to check out the now dead skinbag with Teddy and Dylan. Her hands shook as she grabbed the binoculars from where they hung on her neck and pressed them to her eyes. Like looking through a rain-streaked window, her tears blurred her vision until she blinked a couple of times.

Emily was happy. She deserved to be happy. It just hurt so much to watch the casual way the married couples hugged and said good-bye, like the other was just going off to work. Just as she'd said good-bye to Mitch and he'd only come back as the undead. Nothing should be casual anymore. Nothing.

She turned slowly as she scanned the area and listened to Emily use the walkie-talkie to tell the other watchers to be on lookout for skinbags slipping through the hum's perimeter. A fire sent a small wisp of smoke into the air to the far south. A coyote slipped through the trees much nearer the compound, stalking a wild pig. Seth appeared, running to Teddy's location and the coyote high-tailed it deeper into the trees until a high squeal revealed the winner of that contest. Nature was taking back the abandoned spaces. A bobcat had been spotted in a tree a couple of days ago.

To the southwest, the street ran in front of the RV yard. With most of the nearby trees removed and the houses burned to the ground, Michelle could see past the hum's perimeter, marked with red spray paint on the asphalt. A group of zombs stood just beyond the line. One took a step over the line, and then turned, stumbling back into the group, knocking some of them to the ground.

She took the binoculars off and handed them to Emily, pointing in the direction she'd been looking.

"The hum line seems to be holding. So how did the thing down there get through?"

Her friend looked for a moment and nodded her head before handing the binoculars back. "You're right. Nothing is coming closer." She turned to look at her husband in the field. "I guess we'll have to wait to find out. They don't look like they are coming back anytime soon. Unless you want to go down there and hear whatever they are talking about?"

Michelle put the binoculars' strap back over her neck and let them fall to her chest. "I think I should stay up here and keep watch, at least until Dylan gets back inside."

Her friend's arm came around her shoulder and pulled her in tight. The sigh Emily gave said it all, even if she didn't say a word. She was hiding away, thinking she was safe and cozy in the compound. It was all just an illusion and someday she might be forced to make a choice. A shudder ran down her spine. She tried to hide from the thought in her mind that even then she might not be able to make the right choice.

* * *

"Mr. Teddy, can you take the gun, please."

He took the gun and put it in the holster as little Dylan's body convulsed and he leaned forward to throw up his breakfast. Tears streaked the small, pale face.

"I'm sorry. Now the others will think I'm a wimp."

Taking a step backward from the stinky mess, Teddy reached for his handkerchief and gave it to the kid. He wanted to laugh at the sorry look on Dylan's face but it would just upset him more.

He set the child down on his feet and squatted in front of him. "Even if the skinbags are dead now, they were once people. They were mommies and daddies and kids. We should always feel something when we have to kill them."

Dylan's dark eyes widened as he looked at him. "But you come back from zombie hunting all happy, like you had fun."

Teddy put his hand on the little one's shoulder. "Let me tell you a secret. At first I thought it was fun. Until I had to kill a lady who looked just like my momma, and then I threw up just like you just did. Then it wasn't so much fun no more. But we have to do it. So I laugh and smile when I come home because I'm home. Another day of the zombie apocalypse and I'm safely home with my friends."

"Can I tell the others you aren't big and bad?"

He smiled and cupped Dylan's face. "Let's keep that just between us, okay?"

The little boy nodded as Ripley reached them.

"Mr. Seth. Mr. Seth. I killed my first zombie," the boy piped up. He shot a quick glance to Teddy and his smile faded and a serious look fell on the kid. "I mean. I put down a skinbag because it has to be done. Just a job, you know."

Seth matched the serious look on Dylan's face as Teddy fought and lost to keep a smile off his face.

"Yes, a very important job. Nice to know you can protect the womenfolk and you'll be able to be a zombie hunter when Teddy and I are too old to go out into the wild lands."

He punched the man in the arm. "Speak for yourself. I got plenty of hunting years left in me."

Seth winced from the punch and spoke up, changing the subject. "Did you check out our dead friend yet?"

He nodded toward Dylan. "Was dealing with some other stuff first. So, let's see how it got through the hum perimeter."

"The hum perimeter?" Seth shook his head and laughed.

"That's what Emily and Mrs. Greggs call it," he replied as they walked to Dylan's first kill.

He sniffed as they got closer. "It doesn't smell so bad. He's freshly turned. Where do you think he came from?"

Seth squatted to the side of the body. He started checking pockets and pulling the contents out and handing them to Dylan. "I know you first tried courting during the Disco era, but you could just call her Michelle," Ripley directed to Teddy.

"She calls me Mr. Ridgewood. I'm just giving her the same respect," he answered, taking the papers from the little boy.

Looking at the papers, and then at the dead zomb', Teddy slapped his forehead. "He's deaf. The notepad has I'm deaf on it and some other notes I'm thinking he used back and forth between someone else. His wallet has a card for The Deaf Learning Center in Oakley. The address is down Neroly Road. Must be nearby."

"Shit," Ripley cursed as he stood up. "We've passed it a dozen times when we've been out hunting. It's in that church down on the corner.

About a mile or so, south of here. We'll have to check it out. There could be more of them in there."

Teddy stared at the sky. "It isn't even noon. We could get a group and take care of it right now."

"I want to help," Dylan chirped, grabbing Teddy's hand and trying to pull him closer.

Ruffling the kid's hair, he smiled down at him. "Maybe next time. This time I need you to watch over your mom and the other ladies."

"Do I get a gun?"

"Not while you're in the compound. But you can stand guard and practice with your bow, okay?"

"Cool," Dylan said as he ran back to the RV yard ahead of the men.

"That little boy worships you, you know? The whole Rogue Vantage does."

Teddy stared up to the two women standing on the wall. "Too bad they couldn't share some of that with their mother."

Seth returned the punch Teddy had given him earlier. "Keep working on that. Some walls are worth breaking down."

Teddy barely felt the punch as he continued to stare. *Yep, some walls were worth whatever it took to break them down to get to the treasure inside.*

CHAPTER FIVE

In less than an hour, Teddy and Seth had rounded up the brother-sister team of Josh and Suz Logan. Paul Luther, the right-hand man for the commander of the compound, joined them as well. These days you never saw Josh or Suz without Paul. Teddy couldn't quite figure out if Josh loved Paul too, or if the man couldn't live without his sister, Suz.

It made for an interesting topic for banter around a campfire, their new replacement for the water-cooler at an office or the back fence in a neighborhood, but he didn't mind the trio having his back. They were a lethal group to have for hunting skinbags. Working in unison without a word needing to be spoken, the three of them had been seen taking out twenty zombs in half as many minutes.

They'd arrived at the church to find the parking lot a zombie central of shambling undead tripping over each other. He couldn't imagine how the one skinbag had found the compound because the rest of the deaf-school kids were just milling around in circles and running into walls until their group showed up. Then it was like someone set off a dinner bell.

The moans and the stench reached him at the same time. The group was riper than their friend back at the compound. Teddy pulled the bandana over his mouth and nose and leapt out of the bed of the pickup truck. Two of them were on him before the thud of his boots finished echoing over the blacktop.

He took care of one with his baseball bat and the other one tripped and fell at his feet. One stomp and he was truly dead as well as his friend. Scanning the parking lot, he grinned as the Logan siblings and Paul had a pile of zombs and Ripley was adding his few to the mound.

"That wasn't even a decent workout," he complained as he dragged his two to the gasoline-scented pyre being built in the center of the parking lot.

A moan sounded from the church building and he whipped his head around. "Some of the kids didn't come out for recess."

Teddy and Seth ran over to the door. A steady thump echoed from the other side. Ripley counted down and he ripped the door open. A zombified boy sat in a wheelchair, his struggling movements in the chair causing the footrests to hit the door.

Straps held the thing into the seat. Seth took one side and he took the other and they carried it to the now rapidly burning pile of the finally dead. Teddy tried to pry him out of the chair, but chomping jaws went for his face and fingers. In the end, they could only splash him with gas and let the flames catch hold.

Suz huffed out a noisy breath. "Men. Always have to make it so hard. You could have killed him first."

He and Seth stared at each other, and then started busting out laughing. Once the laughter died down, Teddy caught his breath at the cry of a baby or small child from inside the building. He swallowed hard. *Man, this job sucked.*

They used rock, paper, scissors to see who would go in. Teddy and Paul lost. He handed his bat to the man and pulled the machete from his belt. Suz, Josh, and Seth split up to check out the perimeter of the building for any strays, although they hadn't seen any on the way here.

He'd had some dicey times as a bodyguard, but hunting zombies was like constant ass-pucker time, as he'd called it back in the before zombie time. Must be what it was like to be a cop. Going into a dark building, not knowing what you would find, took balls. If they ever found a cop left, he'd be sure to thank them.

The light from the open door ended a few feet down the hall. Paul flicked on a flashlight and somehow that made it worse. Shadows lurked in the corners and beyond the flashlight's reach. He used his ears instead to be on alert for moans, shuffling of feet, or other out-of-place sounds.

Besides the child's wailing, the building was silent. Paul took the lead as they reached the main part of the church. A giant cross hung on a wall behind the altar. Teddy crossed himself without even thinking of it as they moved to the aisle. The pews sat empty except for dust bunnies blowing across the wood expanse. Stained-glass windows cast a rainbow of colors across the room.

He jumped as the cries echoed from a doorway on the other side.

Paul swept a hand through his hair and whispered, "Shit. I hate this. This is not going to end well."

He had to agree. If there had been anyone alive, they would have hushed the child by now. The odds that they would find a live, uninjured child were too small to contemplate. With a shaking hand, Teddy reached and opened the door. A small girl sat just beyond the doorway, tears streaking down her dusty-brown face. A tiny hand cradled her arm. An arm with a giant bite mark. Something had taken a bite down to the bone. Black lines ran from the wound, down her arm, and the flesh was turning a dusky gray. Her brown eyes were opaque with a milky film. Her huffing breath carried a rotted scent.

"Oh, baby girl," he cried. "Come to Teddy. Let me look at that."

He held out his arms and gathered her to his chest. "What's your name?"

"Phoebe," she managed to get out between hiccupping cries. "Where's Michael? He went to get food. He promised he would be back."

Michael had to be the fresh undead back at the camp. "I'm sure he's around here somewhere," he lied. "We'll find him soon. He took in a large, shaky breath.

"Phoebe, I'm so sorry," he gritted out as he grasped and twisted her delicate neck until it snapped.

Bile rose in his throat. Swallowing it down, he refused to further befoul the sanctity of the church he'd desecrated with his sin of murder. He gathered the small body and handed his machete to Paul. A quick glance around and a short listen proved the little one had been the only one left.

He made it to placing the body on the burning pile before he turned to the side and threw up everything in his stomach. Dry heaves left him still bent over when the others returned from scouting the area.

Pressing on his knees, he stood straight and walked across the blacktop away from the group. What he'd told Dylan this morning was true, anyone could lose it, but that didn't mean he wanted to stay there and have Josh or Seth joke about it. He still felt too raw. Something was terribly wrong in a world where killing that little girl was the right thing to do. He would worry about going to Hell for his sins, but they were already there.

He stared at his big hands. Was it a blessing they were strong enough to end her life quickly or a curse that he could do it at all?

Tears blurred his vision until the big yellow school bus was close enough to see even through the wetness.

* * *

An enormous black man stood in front of the bus as the driver hit the door release and Billy Joe Bennett hopped out. The man was built like a football linebacker. *What diversity he would add to the new, better gene pool. He could rise up a holy army with him as breeding stock.*

He slid to a stop as four guns and a rifle came up and pointed at him. His breath caught at the one female in the group. He would love to add her to the congregation. She looked like a Barbie doll, but the glare and the steady gun looked like Special Forces Jane. This was no meek lamb led to the slaughter. She'd be one of those women you beat to death and she'd still curse you to her dying breath.

One of the men held a hand up. The others relaxed slightly, but left the guns pointed in his direction. His bearing screamed former military. The man put his gun in a holster and stepped forward.

"Hi, I'm Paul Luther. We were just cleaning out this church. What brings you this way?"

Like a good televangelist, Billy Joe could assess a situation quickly and bring the right persona to the table, from humble and begging for money for the poor to ranting and screaming of the coming of End of Days. One truck, five people, no permanence to the church location. They were a smaller group, part of a larger one. He may outnumber them, he may not, but until he got more details, he was going with honest for this encounter. Or as honest as he got.

"We saw the smoke from the highway. We're looking for a location to set up our church. When we saw this building, it was like God spoke to me. Told me, 'you're home.' But we will move on if you have claimed this place first."

Luther shook his head. "No, we were just killing some skinbags. We have a location further down the road a way."

The brown eyes glinted hard as the man kept his cards close to the chest and gave nothing away. Billy Joe pulled out all the charm he was capable of. He reached and shook the man's hand between his two.

"I'm Reverend Billy Joe Bennett. But you can just call me Billy Joe. We would love to use this wonderful church, if no one minds."

The man swung his hand and the others moved forward. "This is my wife, Suz Logan and this is my husband, Josh Logan."

His disgust must have shown on his face as Luther's face twisted into a calm rage he held in check. Billy held his hands up in front of him. "Hey, I do not wish to impose my morals onto others, unless they wish them. But this is why the old world has fallen. We are all in sin. Some more than others.

This new world demands we live the way the Bible has told us to live." *This group is steeped in sin. This is why the world fell. I will cleanse them, one way or another.*

"You can keep your morals and your Bible. This new world is what we make of it," the man said, hatred glaring in his eyes.

"This is Seth Ripley and this big guy is Teddy Ridgewood," Luther finished up in a harsh tone and spread his arms. "The building is yours. Nothing left inside, but you might want to repair the fence to keep out the skinbags."

"No need," Billy said as he smiled. "What others are calling zombies and other wicked, uninformed names, we believe are the Resurrected. They will protect us. The Bible has told us so. Did it not say the dead would rise?"

Luther shook his head. "Whatever. We are down that road over there. I'll tell Commander Jack Canida about your group. I'm sure he will visit you soon, if that is okay?"

Billy kept his smile plastered on his face. "We have nothing to hide. We will count it as a blessing to greet your Commander Canida and look forward to his visit. Perhaps we can visit your group as well?"

Luther stood still as a statue, anger radiating off of him like heat from a furnace. "That will be between you and Jack."

As soon as the truck headed down the road and passed out of sight, Billy turned and yelled to the bus. "Roberta, get your ass down here, right now."

His wife jumped from the vehicle and ran to his side. Her head bowed as she stood there. He made her wait, the tremors in her shoulders an erotic sight better than total nudity of her more than forty years, overweight and sagging body. Walking behind her, he breathed on her neck. Her body twitched. The beating last night had proved women need discipline. He should have started sooner. He would be sure to beat her regularly.

"Go into the building and make sure it is safe for me to enter. See that it is suitable for our and God's purposes."

"But—," she stuttered and stopped.

He leaned closer and bit her neck until he tasted the salty, coppery blood. A whimper escaped her split lips.

"Don't make me ask again."

She ran, tripping over her feet to the open door.

He licked his lips, tasted warm blood, and grinned.

He paced as he waited for her report. Not that it mattered. This would be their new home no matter what she found. His glance turned to the road the truck took.

They would be friendly. They would trade goods and services. They would show they were to be trusted, to be allies. And then . . .

The cleansings of evilness would soon begin.

CHAPTER SIX

Rule #3 *Men aren't the simple creatures we think they are. Some have depth and layers and a way to worm their way through your carefully built walls. Always be on guard, walls are there for a reason.*

Michelle stood on the scaffolding at the front gate. Dylan jumped up and down as the blue pickup truck came down the road. She put her hand on his shaking shoulder. "Please stop that. I don't want to have you break an arm or leg."

"Fine," he muttered, still hoping from foot to foot.

As the truck reached the red line on the road, they slowed and gave two short beeps and one long one of the horn. She took a deep breath she hadn't realized she was holding as the tightness in her chest eased. The signal let the compound know they were friendlies and they could safely open the gate.

Teddy jumped out of the bed of the truck as soon as it braked to a stop in front of the compound. For an instant, he wore a serious look on his face. His gaze shot upward to her and Dylan on the wall and a smile appeared. Like a mask, it covered the sadness she had been sure she saw in his eyes just a second before.

The gate slid open silently on well-oiled tracks. Dylan rushed down the stairs and ran to the big man. Teddy scooped him up and threw him in the air. The child's laughter floated on the air. Michelle walked down the stairs and halted to a stop in front of the man with the boy in his arms.

"How did it go?"

For a second, the smile slipped and she felt she saw the real man behind the fake grin he showed everyone. All too soon it was plastered on his face again.

"Oh, you know. No problem for the King of Pittsburg."

"Dylan," she said to the child. "The girls are waiting for you. You're on lunch cleanup today."

"Oh, man," he whined, wiggling out of Mr. Ridgewood's arms and racing to the kitchen area of the compound without a good-bye.

"Just like a man—whining and bitching about a little chore," Teddy joked.

She wasn't buying it. Her hand reached for his arm and squeezed. "Was it that bad?"

He looked down at her and his Adam's apple bobbed. His lips tightened as he fought to keep the ever-present smile. The smile lost and his eyes darkened as he looked away.

"You don't need my problems, Mrs. Greggs. You got enough on your plate. Those four boys are a handful and a half as my momma would say, along with everything else you do for this camp."

She pulled him to a pair of chairs in the corner, away from the bustling group crowding around the rest of the group that had just returned, waiting to hear about the latest zombie scuffle. Teddy would tell her what happened, or Emily would later with info she got from Seth. The long worried faces of all didn't promise any good news. But news from those who went outside was all she got. It wasn't like there was newspaper delivery anymore or even TMZ.

As usual, he waited until she sat before he took a seat as well. His hand reached for hers and she squeezed his fingers and waited for him to talk—or not. She could talk with Emily later if it came to that.

A harsh cough brought her attention back to Mr. Ridgewood. The words tumbled out like a broken dam, a trickle at first until he rushed through them as if to purge his heart and soul of ugliness.

Was there anything unusual?" she prompted as his words turned to mumbles and indecipherable ramblings.

"No. Some skinbags walking around a parking lot. Then we heard knocking."

He looked away and she reached and cradled his hand between her two. His skin radiated heat through her palm to her arm. It was like an oven to sit near the man, even with the chill in the wind.

"A kid in a wheelchair. No, a zombie in a wheelchair was hitting a door. We got rid of him and then we heard crying. Like a baby."

The air whooshed out of her. Bile rose in her throat. This was why she stayed behind the walls. Inside her motor home. Wrapped in her bed with blankets. The new world was too harsh, too demanding, and too sick. Too much. How much until they broke?

"A baby girl. An itty-bitty thing. Something bit her. I couldn't let her turn. I couldn't. I just couldn't. I killed her."

The words fell in a tumble and Teddy hung his head down. Her heart cracked with a snap in her chest. Tears blurred her vision as she released his hands and he pulled back as if she'd condemned him. Reaching, she cupped his face in her palms. He raised his head and all she read there was a soul-wrenching ache, a need for forgiveness. Lines bracketed his tightened lips and his brow furrowed with doubt. A gray tinge hid just beneath the darkness of his skin.

"You listen to me, Teddy. That little girl was in pain. It would have only gotten worse. You saved her from that. I'm sure you made it quick and painless as possible. You are a good man, Teddy. Do you hear me? A good man."

His eyes widened at the same time she realized she'd finally called him by his first name for the first time. She laughed and leaned closer as her lips brushed his. The man was as still as a statue, until his lips warmed under hers. Her breath caught as he kissed her back. Her heartbeat raced as the moment deepened from a gentle brushing of lips, a benediction, to a warm gliding attack on her senses, and deep in her heart. Her mind said stop and her passions said shut up.

Her fingers slid along his smooth cheeks and reached for the back of his neck to hold him there. The flesh there was hot and smooth as glass. The kiss tasted of his sweat and her tears.

Teddy moved back and her vision took a second to straighten. A real, relaxed smile graced his face, one she hadn't seen in a while, since he'd first arrived at the RV yard. She smiled back; he had that kind of air of happiness that made you want to join in. His eyes twinkled and heat pooled in her chest and between her thighs. They held a promise that echoed the fire of his kiss.

"Michelle. I may call you Michelle, right? You did call me Teddy." He laughed and she joined in. "Not that that wasn't the nicest kiss I've had, but I do have to ask why."

"Why?" Her voice dropped down to a tone she didn't like, the one her friends called the Ice Witch, but she couldn't help it. "I can't just kiss you because I want to?"

"Sure you could. But you haven't even seemed to know I existed before today. So, I have to ask myself, 'why today'?"

She stood up and folded her arms across her chest. "If you think I didn't notice you, you're crazy. Hell, I've seen you in your boxer briefs. You're a little hard to miss with all that."

As she waved her arms around, indicating his body, Teddy stood up and hugged her in his embrace. His laugh rumbled his chest beneath her cheek.

"You're hard to miss, too, Michelle, ma belle."

She giggled. *What was with that? She never giggled. That was for the cheerleaders and hair-tossing flirters of the world.*

"My dad would sing that song to me."

"I may be older than you, but I am not old enough to be your father. Okay, in my 'hood I might be."

She smacked his arm. "Teddy Ridgewood, you are not old enough to be my father. My dad would have been sixty-six this year if the flu hadn't killed him. He was probably old enough to be your father."

His hand reached out and cupped her cheek. He leaned down and his lips found hers. If the other kiss had been hot, this one was scorching. Her face heated up and she grew lightheaded from it. Her hands grabbed his rock-solid forearms and held on. Her stomach flipped like it did on a roller coaster and she went with the exhilarating ride. Who knew a kiss could do all of that?

* * *

He didn't know what had changed her mind and he didn't care. A blast of cold air blew across the yard and skimmed over his bare head, the only area of his body to feel the chill. The rest of his body was fever-hot on every inch that Michelle was pressed against.

Teddy hated to drag himself away from this moment, but he still needed to report in to Jack and give his impressions of the church clearing and Reverend Billy Joe Bennett. Like a dash of ice-cold water, his mind couldn't escape the slimy ooze of Bennett. It wasn't just what he said. It was all that went unsaid but peered out of his ice-cold eyes. Like a vulture waiting for the prey to die.

Her arms dropped away and Michelle backed up. "What?" Her eyes were still hazed over with lust and he wanted to be nowhere but back in her arms to see where this newfound attraction led.

"I hate to do this," Teddy stumbled for words. "But I need to talk to Jack about what we saw out there and I get this feeling that ten minutes from now you'll regret kissing me."

She stood tall and smiled up at him. "I only have one regret in this life, and kissing you isn't it."

His heart was fit to burst out of his chest as she took his hand and they headed to the center of the compound where Jack and Paul were already holding a group meeting. The words 'Bennett' and 'church' filtered through his happy bubble and just like that they were back in the crappy world of zombies and possible renegades. He'd missed the insanity of General Peters and his zombie army attacking the group, but intuition told him Billy Joe Bennett might be just as bad.

CHAPTER SEVEN

Michelle folded clothing on the picnic table as the front gate rolled open and Commander Canida left to talk with the church group. He had Paul and Suz with him as backup. More of the men had wanted to go, but Jack overruled them all with the logic of being less threatening and not giving away their numbers.

She was on the last load of washing when the 'all safe' honking sounded and the gate rolled open again. Three mad faces didn't bode well for the initial meeting. Jack put a hand on Paul's shoulder and the man yelled and shoved it away. His anger carried across the yard even if the words didn't.

Jack marched to the firepit, which had become the hub of communication in the camp. Meetings were routinely held there and gossip circles mingled there as well during the day. He held his hands up as soon as everyone gathered. "We have met with the Fruitful Harvest Church. All I will say is the meeting went as expected. Once the children are in bed tonight, we will hold a group meeting."

Loud mumblings rolled across the space, but it died down as Jack refused to say more and marched to his motor home. The slamming of Paul Luther's trailer door echoed in the suddenly-silent yard.

Dinner was a quiet affair except for the complaints of the children at missing the important meeting. Rogue Vantage sat on either side of her and made their thoughts very clear.

Dylan hit the table with his fist. "We're part of this camp too. We should have our say in what matters."

She hugged him. "I know. But this is a grown-up meeting. I'll tell you all about it in the morning."

"When do I get to be a grown-up?"

"When you are way older than six, stupid," Connor said, punching him.

"I'm not stupid, am I, Mom?"

"Of course not, Dylan." She eyed Connor over Dylan's head. "And don't punch your brother."

"Well, I can't punch anyone else," Connor added with a smirk.

She sighed and hugged Dylan. "Boys," she muttered under her breath.

The boys fought her every step of the way, but she finally got them all settled down in their trailer. Originally, it was Aiden's, but the boys had found paint and personalized it all their own. Dylan's contribution was his painted handprints in a row down the side. Michelle smiled every time she saw them.

Her smile died as she reached the firepit and the angry voices rose. She found a seat by Emily and Seth.

"I think we all need to go to this church," Juan Morales said as he stood from his seat. "Church never hurt anyone, and some in this group could use it."

Michelle gritted her teeth. She'd tried to like Juan but his ignorance reared its ugly head every time she saw him. When she had to gather his bloody clothing he gave her a smile that raised her hackles. She'd seen it before from other men. That "the little lady" smile that implied women didn't have a brain in their heads. Add to that, the man practically strutted when he was down to his skivvies. The picture of skinny Juan thinking he was male model material made her skin crawl.

Paul stood up. "We can't all go. We can't leave the camp vulnerable. I don't think I need to remind anyone of General Peters and the attack on The Streets of Brentwood. I've already stated my opinion of Reverend Bennett and his beliefs. Even if he hadn't stated his morals in stuff that is none of his business, his views of the skinbags as being resurrected people is downright scary. His church may be as mad and crazy as General Peters and his group, or it may not. Perhaps some of us *should* go and form their own opinions, but someone has to stay here and watch the children."

"We want to go to church," Dylan's voice piped up from the open door of their trailer.

Michelle got up and rushed over. "You aren't going."

He stomped his foot. "It isn't fair," he said, marching off to his bed.

She shut the door and returned to her seat. Anger rumbled through the group. "We can take our kids if we want to," Juan complained.

Jack stood up. "We will make a decision as a group on whether we go or not. But the children are non-negotiable. They are the future. They are staying here."

Juan sat down in a huff. His wife, Lila put a hand on his arm, but he shook her off. The woman sat back and huddled in her chair.

Another man stood up. Michelle wasn't sure of his name. "Maybe all the men should go. Give this preacher a show of force."

The women protested loudly until Jack put his hands up again. "An all-male group would look suspicious, like an ambush or raid. We need a mix of the group to go and represent us, while still leaving a group to protect the kids and the camp. You can decide among yourselves who goes and who stays. As your chosen leaders, Paul and I will be going. Thank you."

* * *

"Are you going to the church meeting? You didn't say yes-or-no last night at the discussion," Emily asked as they folded clothes on the picnic table. The rolling of her downcast eyes said her friend already knew the answer before the question was asked.

Michelle folded the baby blanket with precise pressing by her hands. She wanted to say yes. She'd thought about it all through the group meeting last night after Jack and the others had returned with the invitation to the Fruitful Harvest Church.

Going to church would be so—so normal. All she had to do was walk out the gate and get into a truck or car. A shudder jerked her shoulders. She wadded the perfectly folded blanket into a ball and threw it into the basket. She couldn't do it. Staring off into space, she muttered in a small lost voice she hated. "Not everyone is going anyway. Someone has to stay here with the kids after Jack said they couldn't go."

Emily laughed. "Did you see their faces this morning? First time I've seen children upset that they couldn't go to church."

She had to laugh too. Dylan had looked so sad crossing his arms on his chest and demanding to go. The rest of the kids had followed his example when told.

"And what was up with Lila Morales and Jack Canida last night?" Emily said as she smiled.

"What do you mean?"

"They shoot these looks at each other when no one is looking," Emily added. "Did they know each other before?"

Michelle shrugged her shoulders and continued folding. "No one has said anything. Gossip goes around this camp like a whirlwind. You would think if there was something, someone would have said so by now. They can't be fooling around. The commander wouldn't do that."

A laugh across the dirt yard had Michelle glancing up as Beth Evans waddled by with Jed Long, the ham radio operator, his hand resting on the small of her back. The girl turned and laughed with him.

"Has she said anything about them? Are they a couple or not?"

Emily sighed as she glanced over to the young man and woman. "I think she might like him. I know he likes her a lot. But she keeps comparing him to Nick and Jed is nothing like Nick was. Maybe it is just too soon."

Nick had been Emily's zombie hunting partner and the father of Beth's unborn child. He'd been an athlete and the best shot in the group. His death had hit everyone hard. Jed was Nick's complete opposite. A stereotypical, nerdy, comic-book store owner. It had only been six months since Nick's death by zombie. Maybe it *was* too soon. Hell, Mitch had been gone a year now and she still thought of him every day. He haunted her dreams and she kept thinking he would show up at the gate someday. That killing him had been a nightmare she still might wake up from as if it never happened.

She nibbled her lip and her face heated with the thought she wasn't thinking about Mitch every minute of every day anymore. As if she had conjured him with her thoughts, Teddy strolled to the picnic table with a giant grin slashing across his clean-shaven face.

A mischievous twinkle lightened his eyes and his biceps bulged with his hands hid behind his back.

"Miss Emily, Michelle."

"I've told you that you don't have to call me that," Emily chided him.

He leaned down until they were eye-to-eye. "You will always be Miss Emily to me."

"Oh, fine," her friend added as she went back to folding clothes. "Now, what are hiding there?"

He laughed and glanced at Michelle. Electricity shot through the air as his laughter died and he stared into her eyes. A connection was being formed as clear and tight as if a wire twanged, strung between them. "I brought a little something back for Michelle."

She gave him the once-over. His clothes were as clean as when he had left this morning after breakfast. "No zombie hunting this morning?"

"No ma'am. Not a skinbag to be found on our recon. No undead to make dead."

Michelle and Emily both groaned at the latest dark humor making the rounds of the camp.

Teddy continued talking, bringing his arms to the front and cupping something in his large hands. A matted ball of dark fur sat there until it meowed so low she almost missed it. The ball of fur moved and two blue eyes stared back at her and it meowed again.

"His leg is hurt," Teddy explained as he handed it over to Michelle.

Her hands shook as she gathered the tiny kitten to her chest. The front paw bent at an impossible angle on the filthy animal. She couldn't even tell what color the fur would be once cleaned, but the eyes appeared clear and bright blue and it wasn't hissing at her or acting like it wanted to eat her so it was probably okay.

With a yelp and a bark, Nickie, Emily's dog, bounded up to them. The border collie wagged its tail and pushed to see what she held. The cat hissed and tried to climb to her shoulder, the claws digging through her sweater to her skin. She didn't know whether to cry from the pain or laugh at the hilarity of the situation. Teddy seemed at a loss to either pull Nickie back or help Michelle. She started laughing harder than she had in over a year and the cat jumped and bit her on the ear.

It took a few minutes, but Emily got the dog under control and Teddy managed to herd the cat from her shoulder into a rag he wrapped around the shaking animal. "Thank you," she managed to squeak out between laughing and catching her breath. Her skin tingled when he touched her ear with his fingertips.

They came away with spots of blood and a frown marred his handsome face. "Should get that cleaned. We can't be too careful anymore."

It stung as she touched the wound herself. She hissed. "I'll have to see if Dr. Shannon has some hydrogen peroxide. She can look at the cat too."

She took the still shaking cat into her arms and Teddy followed her toward the motor homes. He started for the far row and she pulled him back. "Shannon is usually found at Jim Evans' trailer these days."

"When did the doc hook up with Beth's dad?"

"Last week, I think," she said, nibbling on her lip. "I can't keep up anymore."

"Tell me about it," he added with a smile on his face. "The other day, Paul introduced Suz as his wife to the minister."

"I'm not surprised," she said. "Saw that one coming a mile away."

"How about he introduced Josh as his husband?"

Her jaw dropped open as they reached Jim's motor home and Teddy rapped on the door. She managed to snap her mouth shut as the door opened and Shannon stood in the doorway. Although Shannon was close to her own age of twenty-five, she seemed more mature as a doctor with all the knowledge that entailed.

She was a good match for Beth's father. The man would be a grandfather in a couple of months, but he would be the youngest grandpa she'd known.

He was more than twenty years younger than her father had been.

Glancing over Teddy's muscular body, she realized his age was probably pretty close to Jim's. Neither man seemed particularly middle-aged, able to be a grandfather. When you had to be in shape or die, everyone seemed better than they were before. At least body-wise, her mind too easily traveling to the evil General Peters had perpetrated.

"Need you to look at Michelle's ear."

"What happened?" Shannon directed to Teddy.

He held the ball of fur up toward the doctor. "Cat got her."

"Come on in. Let me take a look." She moved back.

"We need you to have a look at the kitten too. I think her or his leg is broken." Michelle commented as they stepped up and walked back to the kitchen area.

"I'm not a vet, you know," the doctor muttered. She sighed and scooped the cat out of Michelle's hands. Jim was sitting at the table and took the animal from Shannon.

"Why don't you deal with Michelle's injury and I'll take a look at the fur ball here?"

"Where did he get you?" she asked as she opened her medical bag and pulled cotton balls and a familiar brown bottle out of its depths.

Reaching, she pushed the hair back and showed her bitten ear to the doctor.

"Let's see what we have." Taking a soaked cotton ball, she ran it over Michelle's ear. Fire exploded on her skin and she hissed. She bit her lip and muttered obscenities under her breath.

"I wouldn't be too worried. The bite looks pretty small and the cat is probably too young to have a disease." Shannon glanced over to Jim at the table. The cat was trying to walk away over the table and falling over as he put pressure on his injured foot.

"His eyes and ears are clear and I don't see any mange or signs of flea infestation," Jim commented back. "Seems a pity to have to kill him."

Her breath left in a whoosh and her chest caved in like she'd been punched. "You can't kill him. He's a baby." She scooped him up and held him to her breasts.

"Michelle," Jim said in a calming voice that raised her hackles. "He's too little to be without his mother. He needs to be bottle-fed. At any other time that would be a tedious task. Now ... " He shrugged his shoulders like it was a foregone conclusion. "Survival doesn't allow a lot of time for what isn't necessary."

"It is necessary," she huffed out. "Survival isn't everything. If all we do is survive, what are we doing it for? There has to be love, and caring, and pets, and friends, and music, and laughter. There has to be more to live for."

"Well, okay." Jim grinned. "You put me in my place."

"I'm so sorry," she stuttered out, not sure when her mothering instinct had kicked in.

"Don't be sorry. Sometimes we do forget what we are surviving for. Going out there, seeing what is left. You forget we need to carry on."

"Will you help?" she begged. "I have no idea how to take care of a little kitten. Our cats and dogs were rescue pets, already all grown up."

"I'll round up some supplies for you and— have you thought about a name?"

"Yes," she whispered. From the moment she'd seen him she had a name for the little cat. "His name is Hope."

"Well. You and Hope stay here and get cleaned up and fixed up and I'll get some stuff for you from the supply trailer." He turned to Shannon and gave her a quick peck on the cheek. "Get the cat cleaned up and I'll look at his leg as soon as I get back. I'm sure he'll just need a wrap, a splint at the worst."

Jim left and the door banged shut. Shannon handed the cat to Teddy and finished cleaning her ear and slapping an adhesive bandage on it. "Don't take your earrings out until this heals. I don't want to risk contamination in the piercing."

Shannon moved around as she gathered a plastic basin and a rag. With water in the basin, she came to the table and soaked the cloth. "I'm pretty sure we'd all risk injury if we tried to bathe this fellow. Cats are terrible bathers as it is. If we hit his leg, he'd probably hit the ceiling. Can you just hold him, Teddy?"

Bathing a cat was good for a few laughs as they tried to keep the cat still, not spill the water, and watch Hope stumble around with his wet, ruffled fur. Now that he was clean, his fur appeared to be a soft gray.

Her breath caught and tears flooded her eyes. "My dad had a cat just like this when I was a little girl. Her name was Midnight Shadow. Dad said I named her, but I don't remember that. All I remember is that cat following him everywhere. You never saw one without the other."

Teddy reached and his large hand covered hers in comforting heat. "Maybe that will be you and Hope too."

She sighed and stared at the cat. "I doubt it. Once he's healed, he can just slip through the gate or hop on the wall and over, and I won't follow."

CHAPTER EIGHT

"Friends, we are gathered here today to show the hospitality of the Fruitful Harvest Church to the RV-1 group. We are here in this blessed tabernacle, in the sight of God, to show companionship to our fellow members of what is left of the human race. We are here to thank God for his cleansing of the Earth, of its evil minions, of its wickedness, of the destruction of the gift he gave us, of this beautiful Earth and all upon it. For giving us a chance to live our lives right this time."

Billy Joe Bennett bowed his head, the light from the stained-glass windows turning his red hair to flames on his head. Teddy Ridgewood bowed his head to hide the anger in his eyes. The minister and his flock had spewed nothing but lies and deception since their group had arrived for the promised Sunday service.

The morning had started with an argument when they'd arrived with the women in their party. Reverend Bennett and the men with him had wanted to force the females to join their own behind a sheet-covered partition in the back of the church. Commander Canida had refused for all of them and Bennett acted like it didn't matter, but hatred had burned behind those cold blue eyes, even as he slapped Jack on the back and said his country boy 'never minds.'

The service had been just what Teddy expected; a ranting and raving of fire and brimstone for all who sinned. From what he could tell, Bennett seemed to think everyone sinned except for him. Not that you could fault him for the two wives sitting on the stage behind him. All the rules for what constituted a marriage kind of went out the window with the fall of civilization. But while wife number one was probably the original Mrs. Bennett since the Reverend was a good ten years older than Teddy and the missus was as well, wife number two looked barely old enough to date. The hot looks she shot at the Reverend implied they were doing more than dating. The young brunette licked her lips and gazed at Billy Joe like she wanted to take him right there on the altar of a church. On the other hand, the older missus's gaze skittered away anytime her husband glanced her way. Her hand rubbed her neck constantly where a bite showed up clear as day. The woman might as well have abused wife tattooed on her forehead.

Billy Joe raised his head and intoned 'amen' loud enough to echo in the church. The congregation chimed in. Teddy's lips moved but no words came out. He wasn't usually a boat-rocker but he refused to dignify garbage as a sermon. The man's words left a bad taste in his mouth, as if he wanted to spit and couldn't because it was still a church.

He'd been to church as a boy with his parents. A building blessed and filled with singing and faith and love. This one was an abomination.

The wooden pew vibrated as Seth Ripley continued to keep his arm around Emily. Her shoulders shook as she tried to stand up and leave and Seth held her in place. Random words reached him as Emily gave Seth a piece of her mind. Teddy caught the end of the discussion as Seth whispered to her and 'wait until we are out of here' reached his ears. He caught a laugh before it escaped as Emily folded her arms across her chest and glared at her husband.

Jack Canida and Paul Luther walked to the front to shake hands with Bennett. Their leaders had set the ground rules before they left the RV yard. They weren't there to start trouble but they wouldn't back away from it either. Obvious weapons were left at the camp, with knives and guns only carried if they could be hidden. His own gun sat under his arm in a holster and a knife rested in his boot.

He stood up and moved to the aisle to find Bennett there. He reached out and shook hands.

Afterward, he had to fight the urge to wipe his palm on his jeans. Even more so with the first words out of the Reverend's mouth.

"So, Mr. Ridgewood, what do you think of this brave new world of ours? Do you believe there is a purpose to God wiping the slate clean, as it were?"

"Reverend Bennett. Sorry, Billy Joe. I just don't see it. My momma took me to church every Sunday when I was a boy. My God is a kind God. One who loves all of his children."

"We agree there, Teddy. But what about the Flood? Isn't this apocalypse just another wiping of the slate and starting over?"

"Maybe, Billy Joe. But I see the skinbags as more of Armageddon than a simple do-over. We brought the zombies on ourselves, with science and the vaccine, not some vengeful God." Teddy pushed him aside. The man might look him eye-to-eye, but Teddy had a good seventy pounds of muscle on him. He turned his back and helped Emily to the aisle.

She latched onto his arm and squeezed. Pulling him down to her height, she whispered in his ear. "Don't you ever bring Michelle here, you hear me?"

He stood straight. "No worries there, Miss Emily. That woman would have to come out from behind her castle walls first."

Emily shook her head. "Michelle is stronger than you think. When you see someone on the worst day of their lives and they still continue on, day after day, then you know what they are made of."

"You lost Mr. Carl suddenly," Teddy said. "You continued on."

"I didn't have to shoot my husband in the head after he left me to go to work," Emily said. Her face turned beet-red. "Don't you dare tell Michelle I told you. No one knew but me and now you."

"I promise. I won't say anything unless she decides to trust me enough with her story." He put his hand on his heart and bowed his head.

She hugged him. At least as far as she could with that big belly of hers. "You are a good man, Teddy Ridgewood."

Seth coughed from behind his wife. "Can we get out of here now? I've had enough church for one day, and I never thought I'd say that."

Emily snuggled close to her husband as they walked down the aisle to the open doorway.

Feeling a stare on the back of his neck, Teddy turned to find the Reverend and his 'young' wife behind him. A quick glance showed the 'old' Mrs. Bennett still sat on the stage, her head lowered in prayer.

Teddy bowed slightly. "Mrs. Bennett, it was an honor to hear your husband speak today." The words lay on his tongue like burnt rubber for the lies they were. He glanced up, waiting for a bolt of lightning to strike him.

"So nice to meet all of you, also," she replied, arching her back until her breasts threatened to spill over the top of her low-cut blouse.

Teddy stared over her shoulder with heat rising in his face. He'd joked with Michelle about not being old enough to be her father, but he was definitely old enough to be this teenager's father and Bennett had a good decade more.

The man twirled a strand of the girl's hair around his fingers and yanked. She looked up at him and her lower lip pouted and her eyes watered. "Go sit with Roberta and behave yourself, or would you like to join the other wives?"

The underlying tension between the couple vibrated in the air surrounding them. The girl wrapped a shawl around her shoulders, covering up as she rushed to sit on a chair on the stage.

"Women," Billy Joe commented with a laugh. "Such willful creatures. You must constantly remind them of their place."

Teddy flinched as if the man had thrown a punch at him. He gritted his teeth. "And where would *their place* be?"

"Why, at a man's feet, of course," he said, laughing as he turned and walked away.

He shuddered, rushing to leave this place and these people far behind. The damned apocalypse and people still needed to degrade someone to feel superior. They were fighting the skinbags. Why did they have to fight each other?

Spotting Emily, Seth, and Jack Canida, he took a big breath of cold, clean air. Just some people, he reminded himself. The zombie apocalypse didn't pick and choose who lived and who died.

Walking to the cars and trucks, Teddy kept his eyes on the ground as they passed the cages full of skinbags. His hands fisted at his side as he itched to pull his gun and put the poor bastards out of their misery. The moans grew in volume when they walked between. He shook his head. For some reason known only to the undead and the church people, the ones in the cages pushed toward them but the bars held them back and at the same time the ones on the outside pushed against the cages instead of just walking around them and having the group for lunch. He sighed. He didn't know how the repel sound worked at their own camp either.

* * *

"What do you mean the repel sound isn't working?" Michelle slid to a stop at Jed Long's trailer. He and Beth were with the group at the church. She took a deep breath, but before she could talk, Aiden opened his mouth and pointed to a silver filling.

"It's not hurting. The sound is off."

She inhaled and choked on the air. No hum buzzed in a constant bombardment of her ears. The boy was right. The sound was off. Her heart raced in a painful pace against her chest. Over the pounding in her head she heard *them*. The moans of the undead carried through the under-populated camp as they neared the walls. They were pressing against the walls. Their rotting weight against the cinderblocks. Trying to get in.

Trying.

Trying.

Trying.

Aiden grabbed her arm. "Breathe, Mom. We're safe in here. We were in here for months with no repel sound. I think it's just the generator. I don't hear it running either."

No, this could not be happening. She shook her head. "No, Jed filled it before he left."

"Well, maybe it broke."

Broke? She knew what the word meant, but it wasn't filtering through to her brain. Like a hamster running mindlessly on a wheel, her mind turned in circles going nowhere. She caught her runaway thoughts and shoved them away. She could do this.

"Get your brothers and the rest of the kids, Aiden. Put them in the storeroom of the office. Then spread the word to the others. I'll meet them on the wall. Once you tell everyone, you go to the office too."

She held up her hand as his mouth opened to speak. "No, you can't come with me. You and Bryant are the oldest kids right now. You have to take care of the little ones."

"Okay," he mumbled.

Michelle grabbed the boy and hugged him tight. "I'm depending on you."

He smiled at her praise as he turned and ran to do his job.

Pulling an elastic from her wrist, she twisted and secured her hair into a ponytail. At a quick run, she reached her motor home and retrieved Mitch's service revolver. The moans from outside rose in intensity as she neared the outer wall. Her feet flew up the steps to the scaffolding against the gray barrier.

She stuttered to a stop as her gaze swept what had been empty fields this morning, filled with random garbage and tumbleweeds, tossed by the ever-present wind in this town. Her mind saw thousands. Her quick count came up with a little over one hundred and fifty. Sweat coated her palms and loosened her grip on the gun. Wiping her hands, she closed her eyes and counted slowly to ten. As she reached the last number, a pounding vibrated the wooden platform.

Juan Morales ran to her side to look out over the wall. She scooted away. She didn't know the man very well, but what she did know wasn't pleasant. He'd been stranded in a car on the freeway with his wife, Lila and their little girl Selena when Jack and a scavenging party found them a few months ago. The man was a braggart and a bully. She couldn't put her finger on it, but the man just irked her. He reminded her of some of the cops she'd known who took their job home with them. They thought they could control their families just like they had control with a gun and a badge.

"We're here now if you want to join the kids and women in the storeroom."

The other men shuffled their feet and looked away. Heat rose to her face, but Michelle refused to back down to this asshole. Her body vibrated with anger.

"Oh, I think I'll stay. I could use some target practice." Her glare held his. Silent seconds passed until he looked away and muttered under his breath. She wanted to make him repeat his words aloud, but it just wasn't worth it. Something told her he would wait to catch her unawares and alone. Bullies always operated that way.

When he started to order the other men around, she turned and looked over the skinbags below. The scratching of bones and fingernails on the cinderblocks made the hair on her neck rise. She shuddered as they threw themselves into the concrete walls, the thumps ending in a sound like an overripe melon hitting the ground. Blood and body fluids painted the walls below and the stench of dead flesh poured over the wall in waves. They hadn't seen this many in months.

Juan organized the men to space them several feet apart along the scaffolding. Since it was what she would have done, she didn't say a word. He ordered them to fire and the barrage was deafening. As she shot, she wished for the ear protectors she'd worn at the shooting range. She was rusty, she thought as one shot hit a shoulder and she needed another to put the zomb' down for good. Twelve shots, ten skinbags. Not bad, but no need to pat herself on the back either.

Over the sound of yells and guns firing came the roar of racing motors. She lowered the weapon to her side and glanced at the road. Trucks and cars sped down the asphalt. At the red line a horn went off in the approved signal. Juan turned to her. "Why don't you go open the gate and let them know what happened?"

Edward Gonsalves stepped away from firing. He was a sweet man who played his guitar around the campfire for special occasions and the closest thing the group had to a peacemaker. "I'll go get the gate."

She glared at Juan before she turned to Edward. "It's fine. I'll go do it and report to Jack. I'll check on the kids and the others too."

Running down the stairs she felt Morales' eyes on her the whole way. A shiver ran over her skin that had nothing to do with the February wind.

CHAPTER NINE

Rule #4   *Don't trust too easily in the zombie apocalypse. Not everyone is who they appear.*

End of March, 1 AZ (after zombies)
Field outside RV yard

"See if they have any spices this time," Michelle yelled down to Teddy. The field beside the RV yard was awash in color. Red and blue striped awnings covered tables full of canned goods, bolts of fabric, and a myriad of items that before were picked up randomly at Walmart and Target. Things you threw in your cart without even thinking about it. Socks and books sat next to moisturizer and sunscreen. Hairbands and brushes lay tangled with disposable razors and soap. The remnants of the disposable world they'd lost.

"You could go down and find out for yourself," Emily huffed out after climbing the stairs. One hand cradled her enormous stomach and the other rubbed her arched back. "Fruitful Harvest has been setting up here for over a month and nothing has happened."

"Yet," she replied, tracking Teddy's every movement. Every few seconds she scanned the road beyond the field, but the skinbags remained by the red line. Her aching fillings meant the hum was firmly in place. Since the broken generator, her first stop every morning was to Jed's trailer to confirm the machine was working. Her second was atop the scaffolding to view the surrounding area to double-check that the walls still held and the zombs stayed away.

"Since you sent him out there, did you remind him to look for cocoa butter? Unlike Reverend Bennett, I do not believe stretch marks are a sign of true womanhood." Emily's face screwed up as she stared out to the field. She followed her friend's line of vision to spot Bennett for herself.

"He didn't really say that, did he? He looks like a nice man."

Her friend turned away as if even looking at the Reverend upset her stomach. "Last week at the church meeting he smiled at me and pointed me out as the, and I quote, epitome of the perfect woman, breeding and docile." Emily wiggled like a bug ran down her spine. "The man gives me the creeps."

"So, why do you and Seth keep going to the church?" Michelle tore her gaze away from the field. "You can't be enjoying it."

"Seth, Jack, and Paul feel we need to keep up appearances. It's better to know where a snake is so it doesn't bite you on the ass while you're sleeping."

"See what I mean?" Emily nodded her head toward the crowd in the field.

Michelle turned and looked, but she didn't see anything out of the ordinary. Bennett strolled along the booths of trade goods. Nodding and smiling at members of his congregation. You couldn't miss the stern, unsmiling men and the women with their chopped off hair and enveloping clothes. In a T-shirt and jeans she was perspiring on a rapidly warming day.

At first she was sure the woman the man was talking to was one of his own, but the maternity jeans gave her away. Beneath some kind of hair wrap was Beth's beaming face as she looked up to Bennett. Jed stood scowling behind her.

Her gaze shot right and left over the field. All she spotted was caps and hoods and various other head garments on every woman she saw. The few girls walking around were noticeable by their long hair blowing in the warm breeze. But they were little girls, none more than ten or eleven. Turning to check out the camp, she breathed a sigh of relief when she spotted several women with ponytails and braids.

"What in the hell is going on? Why doesn't he just demand burkas? And why are our people going along with it?"

Emily shook her head. "He doesn't demand anything. At least I haven't heard him do so. He just spouts all this Scripture and makes it sound right. That women should want to be honorable and cover themselves. He reminds me of those slick televangelists. You know the ones," her voice deepened and developed a Southern accent as she continued. "God has come to me. You need to give all your money to save me. God wants me saved."

Her laugh died as she gazed on Bennett and Beth with bowed heads and clasped hands as if the man was giving the pregnant girl his blessing. Her skin crawled as the man reached out and rubbed Beth's enormous stomach. Jed's hands twisted into fists at his sides.

* * *

"Look what I've found," Teddy yelled as he tramped up the wooden steps. He stopped at Michelle and Emily's grave faces.

Michelle's face lit up from within and her eyes brightened as she looked at him. A grin broke out on his face. She put her hands on her hips.

"Better not be another kitten. I just got Hope eating regular food and litter box trained so he wouldn't contaminate anything."

"Nope. Better. Cinnamon," he said, handing her the familiar red and white container. Her smile and hug made the K-bar knife he'd traded for it worth it.

"You didn't pay too much, did you? I'll pay you back."

"The only payment I need is the waffles you promised me. Jack not only got some eggs, but a couple of hens and a rooster as well."

She stepped in to kiss him. Her sun-warmed lips slid along his mouth. Her tongue rubbed along his lips and he swept it in to tangle with his. She tasted of honey and tea. His heart pounded as her breasts pressed against him. They broke apart at a groan from Emily.

"Miss Emily, are you okay?"

The woman bent over, her hands clutching her stomach. His breath caught in his throat. It wasn't anywhere near her time and it wasn't as if they could just drive to an emergency room in a hospital. Hospitals had been the first places to become infected. They swarmed with zombs. Even making a scavenger run was tricky; they'd lost six members of their group in a medical run last month.

Teddy heaved a sigh as Michelle jumped in and took charge. The woman may be afraid of the outside, but she wasn't afraid of much else. "I'll go get Dr. Shannon and you get her down the stairs and to their motor home."

He let her run down the stairs first before he moved to Emily's side. "You can do this, Miss Emily." He wrapped his arm around her and held her up. She cried out and blood puddled on the wood between her feet.

"Oh, the hell with this." He scooped her up into his arms and walked down the stairs with care, stopping as she writhed in pain. The coppery scent of blood filled his nostrils and her cries filled his ears. His heart stopped when she lay unmoving in his arms. With relief, he noted the shallow movement of her chest.

He planted his feet as Seth came at a run and slammed into him. The man tried to pry Emily out of his arms. "I have her. Go open the door."

Getting into the motor home and to the bed wasn't easy. He was out of breath by the time he laid her down and Michelle returned with the doctor. Shannon pulled her hair back into a bun and shoved Teddy and Michelle out of the bedroom. He sat on the fold-out couch and hung his head.

"Emily can't die. Not now. Not after living through everything." His ramblings cut off as Michelle knelt in from of him with a rag and started wiping the blood from his arm.

She started to cry and his heart broke. He scooped her up into his lap and held her. Sobs shook her small body. Clinging to him, she wet his shirt with her tears. They both looked up as the bedroom door opened and Seth came out, his face wet with tears and his hands covered in blood.

"Shannon needs rags and warm water. She doesn't think it's the baby. She's not sure yet, but she doesn't think so."

Michelle jumped off his lap. "I'll take care of it. You go on back in there, Seth."

She got a pan and filled it with water. Turning on the burner, she looked over at him. "Go find Mrs. Morales, Lila. Petite, with blonde hair. She helps me with the laundry. She'll find you some new towels and sheets to use for rags."

He jumped out of his seat, glad to have something to do as Emily's screams came again from the back of the motor home. Going out, he shut the door behind him. Spotting Rogue Vantage, he waved them over. The boys knew everyone in camp. They would know this Morales woman.

With Dylan and Connor leading the way, Teddy found Lila and was handed a pile of towels, sheets, and blankets if needed as well. On the way back everyone tried to stop him for news until he growled and they opened a path to Seth and Emily's motor home. He'd apologize later.

He barged in and found Seth cleaning up at the sink and Michelle out of sight. Cries still filtered out of the back but the decibel level had gone down quite a few notches. Seth took the towels and handed them in to the room before getting the pan of water and handing it off as well. The door shut.

Seth collapsed onto the couch and Teddy joined him. "It'll be okay. The doctor is with her. Right?"

"Sure, I think," Seth replied. "She thought it was nothing big. A bunch of medical mumbo-jumbo, but the gist of it was something like a cyst or a large blister. Man, I don't know. Women stuff."

He laughed weakly, gagging at the thought. "Woman stuff, huh? That covers a lot, you know."

* * *

Michelle held Emily's hand and looked away as Shannon finished her exam. The doctor wiped bloody hands on a bright-yellow towel. She swallowed the bile in her throat. Fingers squeezed her hand.

"Hey, you're back with us." Tears continued to fall down her face. Happy tears this time. Color was back in her friend's face and she looked much better.

Shannon leaned over her shoulder. "I've got you all cleaned up. But I want at least three days of bed rest for you. Any cramps, any pain, you send someone for me."

They heard her as she talked to the men in the front of the motor home. Emily squeezed her hand again.

"I'm so afraid. I can't lose this baby. This is God's gift. He wouldn't take it away, would he?"

Michelle swallowed down the big knot in her throat. Her friend had shared her infertility problems she'd had with her first husband. How she thought she would never be pregnant, never have kids. She squeezed back. "You will do what Dr. Drake said. Stay in bed. Rest. Everything will be fine."

Shaking her head, Emily rose up to her elbows. "Tomorrow is church. Something is going on with Beth. I have to go." She fell back with a groan and a wheezing cough.

Michelle shuddered and took a deep breath. "I'll go."

CHAPTER TEN

Rule #5   *You must face your fears head on, or head off in the case of skinbags, because that is the best way to kill them. Fears and zombies.*

"You can do this, Michelle." Emily held her hand and stared into her eyes. "You said you were a Psychology major in college. You need to see this man in his element. You need to talk to the women. I already played my hand. Bennett knows what I think of him but he hasn't met you. You can play quiet and demure."

"Quiet and demure?" She snorted. "I know a lot of people from my past who would laugh at that picture."

Emily chuckled and grabbed her stomach and winced. "I know you don't want to go outside but Seth and Teddy will protect you with their lives. Hell, I've seen you shoot. You could protect them. Only your fear is keeping you inside."

She worried her lower lip with her teeth until she tasted blood. "I know in my head that I will be safe, but in my heart I never want to leave these four walls. I know it's stupid. You've been out there all by yourself."

"It's not stupid," Emily said, squeezing her hand. "You're entitled to your feelings. It is dangerous out there. But life is dangerous. Your husband was a cop. Didn't you know it would be dangerous every time he left for work?"

"He chose that danger and I knew what I was signing up for as a cop's wife. I didn't sign up for the zombie apocalypse."

"None of us did, sweetie. We get what we get and we make the best of it a day at a time. Always been that way. Always will."

"Okay," she replied, sitting up straighter. "But I'm not doing this every week. You get better, you hear?"

"Yes, ma'am."

She was still laughing as she left Emily to rest and shut the door quietly. The humor died like ashes on her tongue as she gazed around the yard and spotted everyone getting ready to head to Sunday services at the church. At least the Rogue Vantage had enough of wanting church-going and stayed quietly at the camp on Sundays. They'd gone once and refused to go again. She'd tried to get them to talk about it, but even talkative chatterbox Dylan just shook his head and walked away.

Anxiety bit into her nerves. She swallowed deeply and closed her eyes. Deep breaths brought the lightheadedness under control. A shadow fell over her eyelids. Her eyes opened and Teddy stood before her. His face freshly shaved and in a clean shirt and jeans.

"Do I look okay?" Her fingers smoothed over the fabric of her one and only dress. It fell to below her knees and just above her socks and hiking boots. She felt like an actress for a Little House on the Prairie remake. She hadn't felt this pure and virginal since junior high.

"Michelle, you look beautiful in everything you wear. But you aren't worried about that dress. You're worried about going outside. Now's the time to change your mind if you're going to go with us or not. No one is forcing you. This is your choice."

She shook her head. "I have to do this for Emily and I have to do it for myself. I'll end up with agoraphobia if I don't do this soon. We've been here six months and I haven't even gone to the field for the trading or shooting practice."

"Agoraphobia?" He looked around at the asphalt ground and the deep-blue sky. "We are outside, you know."

She lightly punched his arm. "Metaphorically speaking, silly. I've been hiding behind these walls and inside these motor homes as if they could protect me. I should know that there is no protection anymore, shouldn't I?"

He clasped her arms and pulled her in close. "I won't let anything happen to you."

She hugged him back. "I won't let anything happen to you either."

Her abundant confidence lasted just long enough for the front gate to start rolling back. The squeak of the wheels along the pavement grated on her nerves. Since the gate only opened enough for one person at a time, they lined up and went through like the endless wait at an amusement park. Her nervous giggle at the thought turned into tremors shaking her whole body. Her teeth chattered like the dead of winter until she clamped her mouth shut.

As they neared the front of the group, her steps grew smaller and smaller and she moved slower and slower. Her vision brightened. The blue of Teddy's shirt blazed in front of her. The yellow of the head wrap on Beth intensified to dazzling sunlight. The red of Jed's sweatshirt bloomed like a wildfire. Her knees locked and trembled. Goosebumps rose on her arms. She couldn't breathe and her vision tunneled to gray at the edges.

Someone grabbed her arms and whispered in her ear. "It's okay. You can do this. The first time will be the hardest."

She opened her eyes wide and saw Teddy in front of her, his dark eyes comforting and warm. His rough hands ran up and down her arms in a gentle caress. Her breath slowed and her heart stopped racing.

"I can do this."

He smiled. "Yes you can."

He took her hand and walked backward through the gate opening, pulling her along in a slow walk. Her breath hitched as the metal grazed her arms. And she was through.

Every instinct told her to run to the truck they were sharing with Jack and Paul in front and Suz and Josh Logan riding in the bed. She turned slowly and took in the area. Only living, breathing people filled her gaze. A few zombs meandered down the road at the red line, but they moved no closer, even with them all outside, even though their moans carried down the street. A sniff brought no rot and decay to her nose. Her ears detected no moans any closer than down the road.

Commander Canida walked over and placed a hand on her shoulder. "Thank you for doing this, Michelle. Seth told us what you're willing to do. Can't say I want to see you suck up to Bennett but he's met everyone else. We need a new set of eyes and ears. Emily says you have some background to help us know whether we should be worried or not."

"If I can pretend to suck up to piss-poor police commissioners, I can do it for one slimy preacher. Although, I'm hoping he isn't as bad as you are all making him out to be."

Jack and Paul laughed and Teddy wrapped a large arm around her shoulders. Warmth filled her.

Not only from body heat, but from their belief in what she could do. For too long, she'd felt like her only contribution to survival was separating the darks from the lights and scrubbing out blood stains. She didn't count patrol duty on the walls since most adults contributed there.

They all piled into the truck. It bounced with Suz and Josh leaping into the back. She took a deep breath as the doors slammed shut. She stared out the window as they crossed the hum line marked in red paint on the street. Her fingers twisted together in her lap until Teddy placed a strong, warm hand on top of her own. They drove slow as men got out of cars from time to time to use crossbows and bolts on the few shambling skinbags.

As they stopped at an intersection, Michelle gazed at the house on the corner. At one time, it must have been a cute house, judging by the roses, overgrown as they were, enclosing the front yard. A zomb' banged against the front window of the house and she jumped. His hands and head left bloody circles on the dusty, smeared glass.

"One of these days we're gonna have to clear these out," Paul commented from the front seat. "They're just a broken window away from being on the loose. Good thing they don't know how to use a doorknob."

"One thing at a time," Jack said, stepping on the gas and driving forward. "We need to know whether Bennett is a problem or just an annoyance. You would think in the zombie apocalypse that the skinbags would be the worst thing to deal with, wouldn't you?"

First, General Peters and his zombie army, and now Reverend Bennett. Why couldn't everyone just get along? Same shit, different day. The ongoing, endless battle of the haves and the have nots. Except, they didn't seem to have anything the Reverend wanted.

She sat up and her mouth dropped open as they approached the church. A banner fluttered down the front of the building proclaiming it the Fruitful Harvest Church in bright-blue paint. But that wasn't what caught her attention.

"What are they doing with those cages?"

Teddy grimaced beside her and took her hand in his. "Those are the Resurrected. Don't call them zombies, undead, or skinbags around him and his followers. For the rest of it, I'm going to let you get your own impressions. We'll talk later." He stopped talking and glared out the windshield.

She looked up and saw Reverend Billy Joe Bennett standing in the doorway with his arms spread wide and a shit-eating grin on his face. A shudder ran down her spine. All he needed was sunglasses and '70s hair to be Jim Jones. He had that same mesmerizing smile on his face. The benevolent-father look, as if he were in his element here at the church.

In college they'd studied Jones, Manson, and the other cult leaders. She'd never understood how people didn't see through them. How they followed blindly. But there hadn't been the apocalypse before. Could the end of the world as you knew it really make you sheep led to the slaughter? It wasn't hard to imagine that lost people would flock together if someone said they had the answer to it all.

Jack killed the motor and turned toward her. "Can you do this? You don't have to. We can just go in as usual and you can sit with us."

She plastered what she was sure was as fake as smile as Bennett's on her face and gazed up to Teddy with adoring, puppy-dog eyes. "Showtime."

He grabbed her chin lightly and got close to her as if he were lecturing her on her behavior. From outside it probably looked a lot worse than it felt. She nodded her head and sat still in her seat until Teddy got out, came around, and opened the door. Sliding out of the truck, she took his hand and stared at the ground as they walked to the building.

The stench of the undead in and surrounding the cages rose up and gagged her. She couldn't have looked up if she had wanted to, the need to pull her gun out of her boot and put them out of their misery would have shown on her face. Her fingers twisted in the soft fabric of her dress.

She was yanked to a stop in front of a pair of red cowboy boots. *Really, red cowboy boots? Did anyone over the age of ten own a pair of those?* Teddy's voice rumbled from beside her.

"Reverend Bennett. Oh, sorry. Billy Joe. I told you I'd bring my woman one of these days."

My woman? An exasperated sign almost escaped her. She looked up and caught Bennett staring at her. With an intense glare, her vision softened and went out of focus. Mitch had once told her it made her look as if she'd instantly lost fifty IQ points.

"This is Michelle. Honey, this is Reverend Billy Joe Bennett."

The man grabbed her hand to shake. "It is a pleasure to meet Mr. Ridgewood's lady friend."

She gritted her back teeth until her jaw popped while still smiling at the slimy man. He gazed at Teddy as if he wanted to start a stud farm with the large man. She trembled when he turned his gaze on her as if he were measuring her hips for breeding and her breasts for feeding the future followers of his cult.

Oh, hell to the no.

CHAPTER ELEVEN

Rule #6 *Trust no one in the zombie apocalypse. The undead want to eat you and the living have their own agenda. No one has your best interest but you.*

Michelle fingered the end of her braid. Trying to not look around again, she forced her gaze on the pages of the worn, borrowed Bible in her hand, but the words blurred as tears flooded her eyes again. Not one woman sitting around her on camp stools had hair longer than a soldier's buzz cut. Some had head wraps like the one Beth had been wearing, although several seemed to be forced to show their chopped hair. One woman had been smacked upside her head when she'd tried to pull her shawl over her head in the frigid church. The spring-like warmth of outside refused to penetrate the dark, cold room.

Desperation and fear poured off the women to flood her with a river of emotions. A plethora of hateful ideas to do in Bennett and his men served to make the preacher's words from the front a bunch of blah, blah, blah like the drone of a dull classroom. Even if she hadn't been so angry, she still wouldn't have listened to his mutilation of the holy word. Every verse was bent to suit his twisted idea of how life should be. She didn't recognize Bennett's God of vengeance and evil doings.

The only thing that would have made this worse would have been suffering through this with Maya at her side. She'd been introduced to the little bitch when they'd come into the church. She'd wanted to feel sorry for the teen bride to Billy Joe until the girl opened her mouth and looked at Bennett as if she'd give him a blow job right there in front of everyone if he'd asked her.

She grimaced as she stared through the gauzy fabric strung across the back of the church. Teddy's bright-blue shirt was a shapeless blob as seen from the *women's* partition of the church meeting. The man was a good actor. He'd had her half-believing he wanted her to sit in the back. Out of sight and out of mind. Put the little woman in her place.

Gritting her teeth, she turned the page of the Bible to keep up with Bennett's pontificating. A small slip of paper fell into her lap. She straightened and unfolded it slowly. Heat flooded her face and her heart raced as she read the simple words.

Help me. Please.

She sat as still as a statue. It might be one of them. It might be all of them. There might be a spy in their midst. Staring straight ahead, she folded the paper as small as she could, bent down as if she needed to scratch her leg, and shoved the paper down her sock, deep into her boot.

Turning another page she found another note. Another page, two more notes. Another page and another note. She gathered them together and stuck them into her boot unread. Turning her head showed every single woman refusing to meet her gaze. She whipped her head back around as Bennett finished and the men shouted 'amen' to the rafters like a movie version of a tent revival meeting. It had that quality of everyone play-acting as if all the talk of a woman's place and men's superiority couldn't possibly be real.

Squeaks and groans echoed from the pews as the men got up. The fabric made it impossible to discern individuals but she spotted a large group in a huddle, with, she assumed, the Reverend in the middle. Deep voices carried back to their location without understanding the words or conversations. The women were part of the church, but yet not.

The slit in the fabric was yanked aside and a large man stomped through. He grabbed the arm of a woman with the remains of auburn hair on her head and pulled her off her stool and to his side.

"Come," he grunted.

All he needed was a fur and a club to make the caveman act complete.

She refrained from rolling her eyes as the pair disappeared through the curtain. That would make a mockery of all of this and it was all too real for those trapped in Bennett's church, she couldn't do that to the women surrounding her. Standing, she put the worn Bible on the stool and started walking to the opening. A gasp sounded beside her. Reaching, the woman stopped her with a hand on her wrist. Michelle looked into her face and the woman shook her head. Apparently, she had to be 'collected' like a child in Sunday school.

She nodded back and waited as the men came for their wives, slaves, whatever they were. Teddy arrived and took her hand. The warmth of his skin and his smile settled her roiling stomach. They were almost done. She could do this a little longer.

The church had emptied quickly as if a task was done and the people had other places to be. Bennett stepped in front of them, forcing Michelle and Teddy to stop. Her heart skipped a beat at the thought of the slips of paper in her boot burning a hole in her sock. She forced her gaze away from her feet and stared at Billy Joe's burgundy silk tie, a useless relic in the apocalypse.

"Michelle," he said. "I'm so glad you could come today. Teddy had told me so much about you that I couldn't wait to meet the woman who he'd decided to make his own."

She looked up and into the big man's eyes. "I'm glad that Teddy wanted me."

Bennett smiled at her and all she wanted to do was throw up on his stupid, red boots. "What did you think of my sermon, about a woman's need to be submissive to her husband?"

She gulped around the knot in her suddenly dry throat. Her answer couldn't be too syrupy-sweet or he wouldn't believe it. She couldn't be abrasive either, or she wouldn't be able to come back again, undercover as it were.

"I think lots of women fight it, but if you are sure of your husband it shouldn't be hard to know he has your best interests at heart."

He smiled at her and a sliver of ice pierced her heart. "But what if the woman doesn't understand why her husband has to do something? What if she doesn't agree with his decision?"

"Maybe that was okay before. To not agree, I mean," she stuttered out. She leaned against Teddy's side as if she needed him for support. "But the world belongs to the strong now, doesn't it?"

* * *

Billy Joe stood in the doorway as Ridgewood and Michelle walked past the cages of the Resurrected. The woman gripped onto the large man's arm and hid her face in his side. He wrapped an arm around her and got her to the truck they'd driven to the church. Her whole demeanor shouted her need for the big, strong man at her side.

A smile broke out across his face as his erection turned to stone in his pants. As soon as the vehicles were out of the parking lot and down the road, he reached and adjusted himself. The thought of the petite and demure Michelle had him heading inside, looking for something specific.

"Maya," he bellowed in the church, his voice bouncing off the walls back to him. The girl was in front of him before the echoes died away. Just proved his point that women wanted to be put in their place. Their hearts knew, you just had to get through to their stupid brains.

"You wanted me, Billy Joe?" Her soft voice and bowed head had him straining against his zipper.

He gritted his teeth and grabbed her chin in his hand. Her dark eyes stared back at him with a fire deep inside, one she tried to hide from him. He was going to beat the will power out of her, even if it killed her. Showing her who was boss was fundamental. He could always get another wife. Michelle's gentle eyes and sweet face filled his mind. He chose to overlook the large black man who'd already claimed her as if he didn't exist. As the woman had said, the strong were in charge.

"Get to our room. Tell Roberta to see to my lunch personally. We won't be leaving the bed anytime soon. We are going to fulfill God's word and be fruitful and multiply."

"Yes, Billy Joe," she whispered, turning and running out of the church as if Satan himself were after her. He smiled. Maybe he was. The world demanded equalization. For good, there was evil. For God, there was Satan. If he were God, he could be Satan too.

He followed more slowly in her footsteps. He'd allow Roberta time to be gone from their rooms. Even the thought of his first wife was enough to deflate his sex drive and his erection. The last time he'd taken her to bed he'd spotted silver among the dark strands of her hair. If she hadn't reached the end of her child-bearing years, they were coming soon. Just the idea of putting her in the cages of Resurrected and taking several new brides gave him back the hardness in his pants, plus a little more.

He opened the door to their rooms in what had been the church's offices. Light filled the space from lamps on several tables. The room had no outside windows, just four yellow walls and a doorway to a back room for the wife he wasn't using each night.

Locking the door, he turned to Maya. She sat on a stool in front of a dressing table. The reflection of her pale, naked flesh filled the mirror. Brushing her hair as he'd taught her. The glossy brown tresses fell to her waist. A vision filled him of a long, brown braid as thick as his wrist. One that had been glossy and shimmering in the pale light of the church.

"Braid it," he demanded in a loud voice.

She jumped, but put the brush down and grabbed a hair tie. Her fingers fumbled with the long strands. "I've never braided my own hair."

He came over and took the hair tie from her. "I'll do it."

His breath came in heavy pants as he divided her hair into handfuls and twisted them into a thick, heavy braid. If he didn't get out of his pants soon, he was going to split a seam. He pulled the young woman into his arms, one hand pulling the braid and forcing her head back. His mouth came down on hers, his tongue sweeping into her mouth. Behind his closed eyes he saw Michelle as she'd stood in front of him, trembling at his maleness.

He shoved Maya onto the bed. Her pale arms reached for him. "Turn around. On your hands and knees."

Confusion flooded her eyes. "I don't understand."

He heaved a sigh and positioned her body. Ripping off his clothes, he groaned as he gazed at the female on the bed. Her plump ass faced him, her wide hips just right for grabbing. He put a hand on her head and shoved her face in the bedspread. He found her opening, wet and ready. Thrusting and slamming himself into her, he laughed as he wrapped her braid in his fist and pulled her head back.

Her cries and then moans fed his hunger. He closed his eyes and fucked her.

Michelle. Michelle. Michelle. Her name a mantra in his head, faster and faster, to match his movements on the girl in the bed.

CHAPTER TWELVE

Rule #7   *A day that starts crappy can end great and unfortunately, vice versa. Each day in the ZA is a crapshoot.*

"What do you mean we can't help them? I showed you the notes. Didn't you read them? You wanted my opinion. That's what I went for, to get my views. The man is a lunatic and those women are in danger. It's as bad as a cult and they are his prisoners." Michelle tightened her hands into fists and pounded the table. Teddy sat at her side with Jack and Seth facing her on the other side. She'd tried to keep her voice down since they were in

Seth's motor home and Emily still rested in the back bedroom.

"Michelle," Jack said. "I'm not the law. We aren't the law. We can't go storming into someone's safe haven and demand they let their wives go, no matter how they are treating them. You heard the Governor on the radio last week. Max Rivers is organizing in Sacramento. He's trying to pull California back together."

"They had a government and law enforcement in the 1800s, but people still protected their own," she argued.

Jack's voice lowered. "I will protect our own to my dying breath. But I can't and I won't go to war with another group that's done nothing to us. We don't have to agree with their beliefs but we have to respect that they have them. This is still America."

She opened her mouth to speak but the commander put his hand up.

"I've said no."

Rolling her eyes and pouting wouldn't get her anything, but she sure wanted to do it right about now. It sucked that Jack was right. Their hands were tied. All she wanted to do was rush out of there and bring justice raining down on the poorly-named Fruitful Harvest Church and they didn't have the right to do it.

"Fine," she huffed and jerked her hand away from Teddy. She slid off the bench seat and headed for the door. Out of the corner of her eye she saw the large man get up too but she didn't wait. She only eased the door shut out of respect for Emily;

otherwise she would have slammed it to vent her frustration.

Before she'd managed three steps, Teddy was at her side. He grasped her shoulders and turned her. Pulling her in close, she was enveloped by his unique sandalwood and man scent. She refused to break down in public, for all to see. She'd always been a poor loser, but never with such high odds as someone's life.

"It sucks to see what's wrong and be unable to make it right."

She looked up as Teddy's voice rumbled through his chest. "Are you reading my mind? That's not fair. I can't read you at all."

His hand reached for her cheek, his warm fingers tracing the angry tears on her face. Eyes as dark as midnight gazed back at her, with a fire burning deep inside. Her palm rested on his chest, the heartbeat pounding against her hand.

"Can't you?"

"Oh," she whispered. Desire for this man flooded her body. Her fingers tingled everywhere they touched him. His smooth skin. His warm flesh. Warmth pooled in her belly and wetness dampened between her thighs. Teddy seized each day like it was a present. Something to be opened and enjoyed right away. The thought of opening his clothes and enjoying him right away had her face on fire. The fire grew into an inferno as he cupped her face and leaned down, his lips sweeping across her mouth. His tongue teased and entered on her gasp. He tasted of coffee and cinnamon and sweet syrup.

She surrendered to the feelings rushing through her. The problems of the world would still be there tomorrow. Today seemed to be a day of seizing her place in the world they faced. She'd gone outside and lived to return. With a lot of help from this man, this gentle giant, who astonishingly, wanted her. She arched her back, pressing against him. He moaned into her mouth. Wanted her as much as she wanted him, evidenced by the bulge in his pants.

"I want to take you to my trailer and my bed, but Miranda and Cody are with me."

She took his hand and pulled him toward her motor home. "Come with me."

Teddy slammed the door shut behind them. She shook her head. In a daze they'd managed to get to her home and inside. She fell into a chair to pull off her boots and socks. Teddy moved her hands away.

"Let me," he said as he knelt in front of her.

Her mouth went dry as he lifted the hem of her dress to her thighs. His calloused fingers trailed down her legs, bringing shivers to her body. She sat back as he removed her boots and her socks, rubbing and massaging each foot. A moan escaped her as his hands left her bare feet and wandered up her calves, over her knees, and to her thighs.

Pulling her braid over her shoulder, she removed the ribbon she'd tied there this morning.

"Please, let me," he said as he pulled her down to his lap and turned her around.

She straddled his thighs as his fingers loosened the braid, untangled the strands, and massaged her scalp. He moved the hair to the side and kissed the nape of her neck. She groaned as sensations pounded into her center. Her fingers reached and gripped his thighs as his lips found her ear, planting small, hot nibbles on the lobe, his teeth grazing her pearl studs.

"Do you like it soft and gentle or fast and rough?" he whispered in her ear.

"I—I don't know," she stuttered. "There was only Mitch."

"Well, I like it sometimes gentle and sometimes rough, but I have to be honest, Michelle, I've wanted you for a long time and I don't know if I can be gentle today. I might want to take you fast and hard until you scream for the whole camp to hear."

His hand traveled up her thigh until it rested on her wet panties. His fingers ran up and down the damp fabric. His other hand grabbed a handful of hair and pulled her head back, forcing her back to arch and a moan to escape her.

His mouth scorched a path of heat down her jaw to her neck and her shoulder.

She groaned in sexual want and her center flooded where Teddy's hand rested on her. Her body moved, wiggling against him, wanting Teddy inside her.

"Do you want me as much as I want you?" he demanded in a husky voice as his fingers moved her panties aside and slid into her wet folds.

"Yes," she whispered as she bit her lower lip.

"What do you want?" he asked as his fingers sped up and pushed her toward the edge.

"I want you to fuck me," she cried out as the orgasm slammed into her, pulling her deep into the undertow. Her fingers dug into his thighs, holding on for the ride.

Her breathing slowed as her heart rate returned to almost normal. She loosened her grip on Teddy's thighs as she leaned back and rested on his broad chest. His hands came up to the buttons on the front of her dress. They fumbled until she pushed them aside and undid the buttons herself. She shrugged her shoulders and let the material drop to her waist.

She was braless as she was most days, using a tank top as an undergarment. His large hands splayed across her chest, the heat of his fingers warming through the thin fabric. His palms grazed her nipples and they rose painfully. She sucked in a breath as his fingers found them, running the tips slowly over the hard points.

His hand grabbed her tank top and pulled it over her head. He lifted her as if she weighed nothing. Turning her around, he yanked her dress to the floor. She stood before him naked, the chill air in the room making her nipples stand erect.

Teddy came up on his knees, his mouth level with her breasts. He smiled just before he swooped in and engulfed her breast into his hot, hot mouth.

She circled his neck with her arms and held on. Each suckle tugged and started a chain reaction to her core. His arms wrapped around her and held her up. When she didn't think she could take another moment, he gathered her in his arms and carried her to the bedroom.

He placed her on the bed and stepped back to undress. Her breath came short and shallow as clothing fell to the floor. His chest and abs were rock solid. She'd seen him before when she'd gathered his clothes, but this was different. This was better. She nibbled her lip as the boxer briefs joined the pile.

His erection stood at attention in the midst of black curls on his groin. His muscles flexed as he reached into a pants pocket and pulled out a foil packet.

"You carry condoms on you?" She giggled as he moved across the room. As he neared, the laughter died and lust took its place. Reaching for the condom, she opened it and slid it down on him.

"Please, I want you now."

His biceps flexed as he lowered himself over her. She ran her fingers over his shaved head and kissed him hard. He entered her slowly. His mouth opened over hers. Their breaths mingled. He swallowed her moan as he slammed home.

"Are you okay?"

"Yes, please, more."

He laughed and began to move. Her hands grasped his shoulders and she held on. Lights flashed behind her eyelids, the room began to spin, and tension filled her body. She was so close. Just a little more.

"Michelle," he uttered in a deep, husky voice. "Look at me. Come with me."

And she did.

* * *

Teddy stared as Michelle stirred. Her eyes opened and she smiled at him. She raised a hand and ran her fingertips down his cheek. His gaze raked her body. A rosy blush covered her face and chest.

"Quit staring at me, Teddy Ridgewood. Teddy? Is your name really Teddy? All I can think of is a teddy bear." Her gaze traveled over him. "And you are no teddy bear."

"My parents, in their infinite stupidity, God rest their souls, named me Theodolphus. Teddy seemed an easier choice."

"What about Theo?"

He twitched like a goose walked over his grave as her mom used to be fond of saying. "I had a drunken Uncle Theo. No thank you."

She laughed and looked up at him as voices rose outside the motor home. It sounded like a crowd was gathered on the other side of the thin aluminum shell.

"Don't worry about it. If it was important, one of the boys would be here." As if she'd conjured them up with magic, a pounding rattled the door and a young voice yelled from outside.

"Mom, you and Mr. Teddy need to come out here right now, 'fore someone gets hurt."

He stared at the door and back to Michelle as she started whipping on clothes. "How did Bryant know I'm in here?"

She laughed as she sat down to pull on shoes. "There is nothing that goes on in this place that the Rogue Vantage doesn't know about it."

She opened the door with Teddy at her back. A circle of people filled the area by the picnic tables. A very pregnant Beth and Jed stood in the center. The girl held a knife out toward the radio operator.

"You have to do it. You promised you would." Her scream carried throughout the yard.

CHAPTER THIRTEEN

Rule #8   Never say *the zombie apocalypse can't get any worse—because it can. And it will. Then it will be worse than that. Evil has no plateau.*

"Beth, don't do this," Jed begged the young pregnant girl, his hands outreached.

Her father inched toward her, but a shake of the head from Jed stopped him in his tracks. The man clenched his fists at his sides, his body shaking.

"I told you I would take care of you and the baby."

Her voice rose and carried over the silent, unmoving crowd. "This baby was made in sin. I won't give birth in sin. You have to claim me as your wife. I won't be a whore."

Jed stood tall and advanced on her. "You are not a whore. Don't say that. Nick loved you and you loved him. You told me so. This baby was made in love. There is nothing to be ashamed of."

The mother-to-be stopped him with the point of the knife to his chest. Her hand trembled as the blade shook and ripped his shirt. The sound of tearing fabric was as loud as the snap of canvas in a hurricane in the silence the camp had become.

"Claim me, please. Make me submissive and pure." Her hand reached and pulled her headscarf off. A long braid of shining brown hair fell to her shoulder. She pulled on it and tried to force him to take it.

His hand closed over Beth's and pried the knife from her. He handed it to her father as her eyes rolled back in her head and she collapsed.

Jed caught her before she could hit the ground.

Her gut-wrenching screams filled the air as her body convulsed. Blood and her amniotic fluids gushed down her legs. The coppery scent flooded the senses as the wetness splashed on her and Jed's legs and formed a puddle on the ground.

Michelle turned to Teddy. "I have to help."

"Of course you do," he said, squeezing her shoulder. "Just know it probably ain't gonna end well."

She sighed, staring at him. "I know."

Proving he was stronger than he looked, Jed lifted Beth's limp body into his arms and headed to

Jim's motorhome. Shannon ran ahead of him and held the door open.

She came up to the vehicle to find Emily arguing with the doctor.

"I'm perfectly fine. I want to help."

The tall blonde shook her head. "This is going to be bad. The baby isn't due for four to six weeks as far as I've been able to tell." She looked around the RV yard. "This isn't a medical center here. With your fertility history, I'm doing this for your own good. You want to do something? Get these people away from here."

Michelle squeezed Emily's hand, released it, and looked up at Shannon. "Can I help?"

The doctor moved out of the doorway and let her in. She heard her friend huff out a breath and the stomp of her boots as she herded the onlookers away from the motor home with a deep, gruff voice.

The stench of blood and Beth's screams filled the small space. Jim sat in a chair with a lost look on his face. Shannon touched his cheek before she rushed by to the bedroom, Michelle followed in her wake.

The young girl writhed on the bed, the covers tossed and bloodstained. Jed tried to talk to her, but she turned her face away from him. The doctor grabbed his shoulders and pulled the young man away. "Let me deal with this. You go look after Jim for me. I'll yell if we need anything."

As soon as Jed left, Shannon turned to her. "Help me get her clothes off so I can see what we have."

Her stomach roiled and bile rose in her throat as they managed to get Beth's ruined underwear off. She hiked up the girl's dress and helped Shannon pry her thighs apart. Beth's screams had dialed down to hoarse whimpers. Her head tossed back and forth, her hair tangled across her face, loosened from its braid.

"I can't have this baby. I can't. I'm not claimed. I'm dirty."

"What is she talking about," she asked Shannon. "Jed loves her. I can tell. He's going to marry her, isn't he?"

A flash of disgust rolled across the doctor's face, worse than any she'd ever seen on Shannon's face, no matter the situation.

"Oh, Jed wants to marry her all right. As soon as the baby was born, from what I hear and he told Jim."

Shannon reached to examine Beth and Michelle stared off across the room, afraid to look at the young girl's bloody thighs.

"But?"

"But she's got some stupid notion that she has to be 'claimed.' That she won't be pure until she is submissive and a wife, just like those nutjobs at the church. You saw their women, right? You think they cut their hair off themselves, like some modern day ritual of the Orthodox Church from the ancient past. Hell, no. That's how the men 'claim' them. At least that's what Beth told me and Jim one day after she'd been to see that Reverend Billy Joe

Bennett. They marked them by cutting off their hair."

Shannon sat up and wiped her hands on the covers. "Tell Jed and Jim to boil water and find me as many towels and blankets as possible. She's dilated. This baby is coming today, whether it is time or not."

Michelle left the room and got the pot of water going. She sent Jed to get towels and set Jim to watching the water. She took a deep breath and returned to the bedroom. Beth sat up on her elbows and strained, her face red and covered in sweat. Her lip bled where she'd bit through it.

Michelle went to the head of the bed and placed herself behind Beth, supporting her shoulders and giving her something to lean on. The girl collapsed back and panted in gulps. Her crying brought tears to Michelle's eyes. All this effort in what would almost certainly be a lost cause. Was this what Emily had felt every time she'd thought she was pregnant and she wasn't or she lost the baby after only dreaming of it for days or a week or two? Poor Beth had seven months to think and dream of a baby.

She stepped away from thoughts of babies and dreams and futures. All there was, was now. This just highlighted the point. Beth cried out as her stomach stretched and moved, pressure from hands and feet appearing on the taut skin. She moved and pushed the girl up higher.

"Push, Beth," Shannon yelled from between the girl's legs. "Just a little bit more."

Beth groaned, her fingers grabbing into the covers. Her screams echoed in the little room as a gush of blood proceeded the baby. Shannon worked to pull the baby the rest of the way out. Stark silence filled the room.

"Why isn't it making any noise? Let me see my baby." Beth cried as she tried to reach for what Shannon held in her hands.

Michelle forced herself to look. She girded herself to look at the blue, lifeless body of a baby born before its time. But she gasped and choked, gagged at the gray thing in the doctor's hands. It lay there motionless, and then twitched, its eyes opening, opaque and dead.

"Oh, hell no," Shannon whispered. "Michelle, hand me your knife. Now."

"No, don't hurt him. He's resurrected," Beth cooed and smiled.

The hair rose on her arms as she reached for the knife in her boot. She handed it to Shannon and wrapped her arms around Beth. The girl thrashed and tried to reach for the thing she'd birthed, but Michelle was stronger than Beth, especially in her weakened condition.

Shannon removed her shoelace and tied off the umbilical cord. She reached and cut it a few inches from the stomach of the abomination on the bed. She placed it to the side, and worked to take care of Beth.

By the time she finished and gave Beth a shot from her medical bag the infant skinbag bled out and lay truly dead on the stained and soiled covers.

She turned away as Shannon used the knife on the tiny skull to be sure. Michelle gagged and swallowed against her stomach rising to her throat.

The room looked like a battlefield and maybe it had been with the bloody sheets and the dead thing on the bed. Michelle got up and reached for the doorknob.

"Michelle, tell Jim and Jed the baby was too soon. Okay?"

She nodded. "Of course."

Because what else could she say? We're not going to hell. We're already there.

* * *

Michelle plodded down the stairs from the motor home like a million pounds sat on her shoulders. The bloody, lumpy blanket she held in her arms said it all. Her red-rimmed eyes looked up at him and Teddy wanted to take all that weight off her shoulders and his heart ached with knowing he couldn't. He didn't care what anyone said. Women were the stronger sex, they had to be. How else could they keep getting pregnant and having babies?

"It was still-born. Can you . . . you get rid of it, please?"

He took the bundle with all the care he would have given a newborn baby. His natural curiosity rose as he cradled it in his arms.

Why hadn't she said he or she or even, the baby?

"Don't ask," she said, her eyes refusing to meet his.

"It will be okay," he whispered, wanting to hold her instead of the bloody bundle.

"I'm not so sure," she muttered as she turned and walked back to the motor home. Several people opened a walkway and gave her a wide berth.

At the click of the door, Teddy hefted the tiny load and headed out to the gate and the field across the road. He plodded along until the boys of Rogue Vantage met him at the gate. He shook his head as they tried to exit the yard with him.

"Not today, boys. You don't need to be seeing this."

"We can watch your back," Aiden and Bryant piped up.

He gave them a weak smile. "You watch from the gate, just in case. Give a holler if you see anything."

Trudging across the asphalt his gaze swept over the tidy field with its collection of makeshift memorials and crosses. Not a lot, but still too many. The first row contained the parents of the boys watching his back. Commander Canida told him of finding the little ones the only living beings in the yard. The bodies of their parents and the other grown-ups had been too heavy for the children to move and the skinbags had made it too dangerous for them to dig graves.

The next section held four graves of people with injuries that in the before Z time would have needed a shot of antibiotics and rest to cure. He scuffed his feet in the dirt as he passed the next section with three graves of the elderly who'd died in their sleep and needed to be put down after the turn.

He trudged along until he reached the empty section with a grave already dug, with Jed standing by its side. Teddy stopped and gripped the bundle tighter. "You don't need to be here, bro."

Jed's hands gripped the handle of the shovel until his knuckles stood out against his pale skin. "Yes, I do. I let Beth down. I should have seen it coming."

He knelt beside the grave and slowly lowered the blanket-wrapped bundle into the ground. His vision blurred with wetness as he stood and wiped his hands on his pants.

"Can you say a few words?" Jed blurted out, the tears rolling down his face.

"I'm no minister or pastor," Teddy started.

"To hell with them all," Jed said, his eyes narrowing and his lips thinning.

"Okay, then," he began, lowering his head. "Lord, please take this baby into your arms and keep it safe in your love and protection. Amen."

"Amen," Jed echoed, taking his glasses off and wiping his face with his sleeve.

Teddy reached for and took the shovel, scooping up the dirt of the field and filling the small grave with three or four shovelfuls. He leaned on the tool as Jed squatted down and picked up the tiny cross he'd made of two pieces of wood nailed together. Colorful ribbons criss-crossed and wrapped around it.

Teddy read the etched *Baby Evans-Cruz* as Jed hammered the thin wood into the ground at the top of the mound of freshly turned dirt.

CHAPTER FOURTEEN

Two weeks later

The mouth-watering scent of pork wafted through the RV yard and carried to the gate where Billy Joe stood, his face red and his anger raising his blood pressure. The idling motor of the bus and the sound of irritating voices reminded him he wasn't alone.

Jack Canida and Paul Luther stood on the other side of the gate, arms crossed on their chests. The field beside the encampment stood empty of tents and people eager to trade.

"Like I said," Jack told him in that uppity military tone. "The people of RV-1 will no longer do business with you. You and yours are no longer welcome here. Leave us in peace and we will do the same. Mess with our people again and Hell will seem like a picnic to what we will do to you."

"Now, Jack. I told you I was sorry about that little girl's baby. But I don't see how it is our fault that she lost a baby conceived in sin. Only God talking care of things, as far as I can see."

Paul started toward the gate with murder in his eyes, until Jack reined him back with an arm across this chest, stopping him from going for Bennett.

Billy Joe put his hands on his hips. "That's right, Canida. You better stop your bisexual bulldog before God brings his wrath down on his wicked ways as well."

Jack laughed, his eyes bright and shining. "I wasn't protecting Luther, I was protecting you."

He bit his tongue. He didn't think his face could get any hotter, but now it was on fire. He'd tried to help these sinful people and this was the thanks he got. Why were good Christian people always persecuted? How much were they supposed to take before they snapped?

"I've always just wanted to help. To bring salvation to your people."

"Our people don't want what you're selling."

A scuffle and yelling started twenty feet or so from behind Jack and Paul.

"I don't want to go, Juan."

"You will do what you're told, Lila, or so help me God I'll give that little whore Selena to the first man who wants her."

"Please, Juan. Don't hurt her. She's only eight years old."

Billy Joe stared over Jack's shoulder as Paul grasped the commander's arm and pulled him back. *Now, wasn't that interesting?*

Juan Morales had his wife, Lila by the arm, her struggles doing nothing to throw him off. The man was thin, but wiry. Their daughter, Selena scrambled in their wake, weighed down with a backpack bigger than she was.

He grinned. At least one man in this group knew how to be a man and put women in their place. Locking his fingers together in prayer, he raised his face to the heavens and called out to Juan in a voice that carried over the growing crowd inside the gate.

"Brother Morales, God has shown you the way. The Church of Fruitful Harvest welcomes you and your family."

"We are ready to join you, Billy Joe," Juan called, dragging his wife to the gate and glaring at Jack and Paul. "We're leaving this evil, Godless place, and you can't stop us."

"This isn't a prison, Juan. You are free to leave," Jack said, raising his shaking hand and giving a signal. The gate slid open wide enough for one person to pass through.

Paul turned to the commander. "You can't let him treat her that way. You have to do something."

"I can't. We aren't the law. She's his wife. We don't have the right to stop him." The words were said hard and cold, but the commander's eyes were warm as he stared at Lila. There was something there. Something he would store for later, in case he needed it.

Billy Joe raised his arms. "Only God is the law."

Jack stared at him, those cold eyes probing and dissecting. "I think Governor Rivers and President Thomas would have something to say about that. Doesn't the Bible say, 'Render unto Caesar the things that are Caesar's, and unto God the things that are God's'?"

His face heated again and he wished for a weapon to destroy Jack Canida and his band of heathens. He put his shaking hands behind his back and waited for Juan and his family. Perhaps one man's leaving would start an Exodus of the barbarian camp.

The girl shrieked as the man kicked her out the gate. She fell to the ground, white-blonde hair falling all around her. One of the women came off the bus and picked her up, helping her back to the vehicle. Her cries faded away, drowned out by the yells of her mother.

Her hands latched on to the metal fence until Juan kicked at them with his boots. Her bloody fingers dropped to her side as her husband shoved her toward the bus. Defeat permeated the air around her as her head drooped and Juan placed his fist in her hair to pull her along. She stumbled over the rough road, only her husband's hand keeping her upright.

"You bastard," a yell went up as a woman streaked to the fence. Long brown hair cascaded over shoulders barely covered with a tank top, the rest of her exposed in a pair of tiny shorts.

"Michelle," he whispered on an exhale but she ignored him, her eyes set on Juan Morales.

She stomped up to the man and yanked his shoulder. He came around with a gun in his hand, pointed at her chest. The woman skidded to a stop, the gun's barrel inches from her body.

Michelle sneered at him. "You know what they say about a man and his gun, don't you? Compensating for something, are we, Juan?"

Billy Joe bit his cheek to stop the laugh he might have let slip. The woman was fire and sunlight. Hard as a rock and as soft as a woman should be. His erection throbbed with the rapid beat of his heart. He was going to get this woman. He licked his dry lips and swallowed. His time would come.

The large, black man strode through the gate and stepped in front of Michelle. He glared at Juan until the man's face reddened and the gun in his hand shook.

"You want to put that away, little man, or I'll make you eat it."

The man slammed the gun into the holster on his belt. "We're leaving and you can't stop us."

Teddy Ridgewood leaned down until he was face to face with Juan. His raspy whisper carried to Billy Joe.

"Just know, I would if I could. Don't doubt it for a minute."

Michelle came from his back and slipped under his arm. He hugged her shoulders and squeezed. She smiled up at him and Billy Joe felt the green-eyed snake of jealousy rip through him. His hands tightened behind his back until the knuckles cracked.

I'll have you naked and in my bed. Or I'll have you Resurrected in a cage.

* * *

Michelle shuddered as she glanced over her shoulder and caught Bennett staring at her. Teddy squeezed her shoulder and pulled her in closer.

"Are you cold? You could have put more clothes on to run to the rescue, you know?"

"No, I'm fine." She refused to turn back but she could feel his eyes on her like a gun pointed at her back. "It's just the Reverend."

"What about ol' Billy Joe?"

She laughed, but it died quickly. "Don't make light of it. He is like a skinbag creeping in the tall grass, just waiting to get you as you walk along, all unawares."

"Well, he can't get you unless you go running out of the gate without thinking."

"I did do that, didn't I" She smiled up at him.

He stopped, pulling her to his chest, leaning down and taking her lips in a deep, hungry kiss. "You'll be off zombie-hunting with me in no time," he said as the kiss ended.

"I don't think so," she whispered, sliding her lips across his, not wanting it to end.

She pulled back. "I wouldn't mind hunting and doing in Bennett. The man gives me the creeps. He looks at me like he wants me naked, sprawled at his feet."

Teddy grinned. "That's a nice picture. I'd like you naked, sprawled at my feet."

She grinned back and slapped his arm. "Tag, you're it. Last one to the trailer is the naked sex slave."

Her long strides had her touching the metal door two steps before Teddy. She turned as he pressed her up against the side of the trailer. "I think you let me win. I think you want to be the sex slave."

"But of course, Mistress. Whatever you desire."

His rich, deep voice sent shock waves through her body. His hot gaze drove tremors to her thighs and between as well. His warm hands on her arms delivered X-rated visions to her brain. Her hand fumbled and found the doorknob. They fell in, as she ripped his T-shirt from his body. His chest and abs glistened with light perspiration. His sandalwood scent filled the confines of the trailer as he stripped and came to her on his knees.

"Whatever you desire."

"Strip me," she ordered.

His hands came at her in a rush. She stared into the dark depths of his eyes.

"Strip me, slowly."

His gaze lowered to follow his hands on her legs. His fingers glided down and in slow motion took off her boots and socks. Her panties were wet and she still had most of her clothes on.

His enormous, hot hands took up a foot and caressed the sole. She arched her back and moaned. He slid up her body until his hands were on the button on her shorts. A flick of his fingers and they popped open. He grabbed her hands and stood her up with him still on his knees before her.

He peeled the old cotton shorts off of her with a slow glide that would have done excellent duty for undergarments of silk and lace, on a night of candlelight and champagne.

Her heart beat faster at the thought of all the time in the world with Teddy in a safe place that allowed lingerie and long, slow love-making. She imagined Penthouse hotel rooms and hot tubs to relax in after scalding, passionate love-making. The heat rushed to her face as the man before her helped her step out of her shorts and he tossed them aside. He stretched and grasped the bottom of her tank top. Moving it an inch at a time, his fingers grazed over her stomach and tickled her sides. The thin material caught on her nipples and brought them out firm and sensitive. Her top joined the shorts across the room. With a finger, Teddy pulled on the top of her panties, the tip teasing at the curls between her thighs. Electricity zinged through her body and sent a gush of warmth to her woman's core. Her knees turned to rubber and she placed her hands on his shoulders.

"Strip me."

So slowly it seemed the fabric wasn't moving at all, he pulled her panties down her thighs. He kissed every inch as it appeared. His warm lips and hot mouth on her bare skin sent all the blood in her body to the apex of her thighs. Her fingers tingled as she grabbed onto his shoulders.

She wanted him this second but the game was too much fun. She felt like a goddess, a sexual goddess. Lifting her leg, she placed it over Teddy's shoulder and brought herself closer to his face. His hands cupped her butt and pulled her closer still.

"Whatever you desire," he whispered against her thighs.

Her fingers slid down her stomach and tangled in her curls. "Kiss me. Here. Make love to me with your mouth."

"Whatever you desire," he whispered just before he did exactly as he was ordered.

CHAPTER FIFTEEN

Teddy pushed up from kneeling in front of the tiny grave. The wildflowers he'd planted a couple of weeks ago were putting forth flowers. The tiny white buds covered the little bush. A few torrential rain falls had done wonders for the scraggly plant. A scuffle behind him had him yanking the knife from the sheath on his belt and whipping around. The constancy of the humming repel sound made him relaxed and off-guard.

Beth Evans skidded to a stop in front of him, with Miranda a few steps behind. Although the young girl had seemed to recover from her loss of a baby, Ran had been keeping close tabs on her.

"You shouldn't be out here, Miss Beth." His gaze looked her over quickly. "Hell, you don't even have a gun or a knife."

His gaze shot to Ran and he raised an eyebrow.

"I'm sorry, Teddy. I thought she might like a walk or to get out. I have my weapons. I would have protected her."

"I know you would, Ran," he said. He did know the young woman was every bit as good as a skilled man with her gun and her knife. "But maybe Miss Beth shouldn't be here yet."

Her green eyes filled with tears and her hands clutched at her dress fabric. "I should have been here before now. It's my fault he's dead."

He released a big sigh. Whatever fanaticism she'd had for the ways of Bennett and his church seemed to have died with her baby. She'd woken up mourning the child and wanting her family and friends around her. Her long brown hair flowed down her back uncovered and she was back to treating young Jed as a potential husband. Still, something in her eyes looked broken, like shattered china that could never be put back into one piece. She'd lost that young girl sparkle she'd had.

"The baby was a boy, wasn't it?" Her soft-spoken question pierced his conscience. He hadn't looked when he'd buried the bundle, and he hadn't wanted to. Only Michelle and the doctor knew anything for sure. If this little girl wanted it to be a boy, a boy it would be.

"I'm pretty sure that's what Michelle said," he said, with a tiny twinge for the lie he told.

"You planted flowers," she whispered with a sweet, heartbreaking smile. She rushed forward and hugged Teddy.

He patted her back and let her tears wet his shirt. Maybe they should have brought her out here before now. Might have helped her. Or given closure like all the self-help books used to preach.

Ran coughed. "I'll wait over here by the road."

The young woman trod over the dirt clods and stood guard on the asphalt. He sighed again. Another broken woman, although she'd pulled herself together and come out of the fire, stronger than before. No telling yet whether Beth would be stronger or fall apart at the next catastrophe. Only time would tell.

She moved away and fell to her knees at the graveside. "Can you fix it?"

A shiver went up his spine, just like his momma said, like someone walked on your grave. Had Beth lost it totally? Would she be a danger to others, or just herself?

"Miss Beth, what do you want me to fix?" *Don't let her say the child. Can't nobody fix that.*

"The cross. He should have a name, shouldn't he? Even if he didn't live, he should have a name of his own."

"Yes, he should," Teddy agreed, grabbing the cross and handing it to Beth. She started untwining the ribbons and set them on her dress as he got more pieces of wood and quickly nailed them together.

He brought the finished cross and a thick nail they'd been using for scratching out the names on the wood. She took it and stared at the old cross.

"I should keep the Evans-Cruz. Nick would have liked that." Tears covered her cheeks but a smile lit up her face. "His father was Diego. It means James in English and my dad is Jim, I mean James, too."

She nodded and Teddy scratched *James Evans-Cruz* on the battered wood. Beth twined the ribbons back on and he pounded it into the ground above the small grave.

"If we find some paint, I'll come back and paint his name," she said, her voice stronger.

"That would look very nice, Miss Beth."

* * *

Michelle stood at the gate with her hands wrapped around the metal bars. Teddy and Beth knelt by the graves in their growing burial ground. The row with Beth's baby already held two more gravesites; one was a young man who'd gotten gangrene after an injury and the other was his mother who couldn't go on without him. They'd heard her moans in the motor home she occupied and gone in and made her dead dead.

She brought herself back to the present as tears flooded her eyes watching Teddy make what she assumed was a new cross to Beth's wishes. Her mind turned away from any thoughts of what the girl had birthed and they had buried. She hoped this would end the sad chapter in the young girl's life. Jed was a wonderful man who adored Beth and would do anything for her. Her ears caught the sound of shooting practice from the other side of the walls. The radio operator had taken to learning guns and the crossbow in an effort to prove he could protect Beth. From the smiles she'd seen between them, it wasn't a wasted effort either.

A gust of wind from the north carried the unmistakable scent of rot and decay. It couldn't be a horde, the sound was working, she could tell with the constant hum in her head. Her next thought was of the deaf skinbag not so long ago.

The stench came and went with the breeze. Out of the corner of her eye, she spotted her. An undead female in running shorts and what was left of a sports bra. The earbuds she wore explained it. Although the batteries on whatever device she'd been using were probably long dead, just having them in the ears was enough to hinder the repel signal.

She went to yell to Miranda, but the girl had moved away, toward Teddy and Beth. Their backs were to her and she couldn't yell without alerting the skinbag who was oblivious of them at the moment. Maybe it would just shamble along.

Please. Please. Please.

Prayers seemed to go unanswered these days, as the thing must have seen the group in the cemetery, or caught their scent. Her steps sped up, but no moans sounded to let the group know they weren't alone. Michelle looked around and found no one. It took a split-second to realize it was only up to her.

She rushed to push the button to open the gate and ran out of the opening. Miranda looked up and began to pull her gun, but Michelle was faster.

The pistol bucked in her hand, the skinbag fell to the ground with a hole in its head, and the echo rang in her ears. She shoved the weapon in the holster and whipped around to make sure they were safe.

All of a sudden, what she'd done sank in. She was outside the gate, in the middle of the road. She'd opened the gate and run out without thinking. Her teeth chattered until she clenched them together and breathed deeply. She'd done it. She'd willingly exited the yard. She wasn't going to wimp out now.

Walking toward the cemetery, she met the others by the fallen body. Teddy turned her over with a push of his boot and Michelle saw in an instant why the thing hadn't alerted them with the trademark moans they all used. Her windpipe was gone, hell; most of her throat was gone. She wasn't sure how the skinbag's head had stayed on.

"Why don't you girls get some men so we can take care of this?"

"Girls? You have got to be kidding me?" Michelle put her hands on her hips.

"Really?" Ran added. "I'll go get some gasoline so we can burn this mess." The young woman turned away and stomped across to the gate.

Beth looked from Teddy to Michelle and swallowed loudly. "I'm going to go see if Jed will give me some gun practice so I can shoot like Ran and Michelle."

When Beth turned and left, silence fell over them. Teddy wore that look that men have perfected when they have no clue.

"In case you failed to notice it, and I'm sure you did, high-and-mighty King of Pittsburg, I ran out that gate to save you. I shot that thing to save your ass and all I get is 'you girls.' This is not the Church of fucking Fruitful Harvest and you are not that bastard Bennett."

"Ah, Michelle, ma belle. Don't be that way," he crooned as he reached to hug her.

She pulled back and his arms fell away.

"You said you'd be right back."

"I was right here, you could see me though the gate."

"You promised you'd be right back and then you died," she yelled, the tears flooding her eyes and running hot down her face.

He spread his arms. "I'm not dead. What are you yelling about?"

"You died and then you came back. Just like you promised," she whimpered, wrapping her body in her arms, rocking back and forth as reaction set in. "Just like you promised."

"I am not your husband, Michelle. I'm not Mitch."

She glared up at him and he stepped back. "No, you're right. You're not. He came back like he promised and I killed him."

147

* * *

Teddy stretched out his arm, but Michelle had already turned and walked away across the road and through the gate. It slid closed and locked with a loud clang that carried across to him, like the slam of a prison door, except he was on the outside.

He couldn't help smiling a little. She *had* rushed out the gate. Rushed out to save him. Damn it! He wasn't her husband Mitch. He would never have gone to work and not been there to protect his woman. Family had to come first. His dad taught him that. Among so many other things.

The opening clatter of the gate cut into his thoughts, but when he looked up it was Ran with a wheelbarrow and a gas can. She pushed it over and they got the skinbag into the barrow and he led the way to the side field where they were burning bodies so they were downwind. Ran followed with the can and her endless ramblings. At any other time he loved listening to the girl who could go off on twenty tangents at one time. Now, she grated on his last nerve as she droned on about his failings as a man.

"Everyone knows you don't call women girls anymore. Like, duh."

"Now you sound like Cody. That boy is rubbing off on you."

"Don't call him a boy. He is all man, if you know what I mean."

Teddy found himself blushing. "I do know what you mean and I don't want to. What is it you kids say, TMI?"

"It's so lame when old people try to sound hip." She did the L sign on her forehead with her fingers.

"You're like forty, Teddy. Z days are going to be like the old times, when people died young. It's already happening. We're going to die of colds, and accidents, and heart conditions we can't treat anymore."

That sobered him up quickly. Ran was right. In the ZA he might be an elder. He shook that thought away. Hell, no. Maybe decades from now the live expectancy might be way young again, but he still had a pre-Z mind and body. Flexing his biceps, he dumped the zomb' out of the barrow and yanked the gas can away from Ran.

He poured the fluid over the former female, the fumes rising in the still air. Setting down the can, he lighted a match, tossed it, and stepped back.

"I never get used to the smell," Ran said, grabbing her bandana and tying it across her mouth and nose.

He followed suit. "Me either, Ran. Me either."

"The ZA sucks."

He couldn't agree more. He glanced sideways at the figure up on the wall. Her blue shirt like a bright painted spot on the gray cinderblock expanse. Her glance slid over him.

"Yes, it sucks."

CHAPTER SIXTEEN

Rule #9   *Don't ruin relationships for no reason. In the ZA, someone has to have your back and you have to have theirs. At all times.*

The man trudged up the sidewalk, his gait shambling and stumbling. The once-pristine uniform caked with blood and gore. She raised the gun to shoot and the uniform changed to jeans and a T-shirt, Mitch's face changed into Teddy's. Her finger tightened on the trigger and she pulled. The man fell to the ground, not breathing, not moving.

Michelle jerked up out of sleep. Her heart pounded in her chest, the whoosh of blood thumped in her ears. She pushed her sweat-drenched hair off her face. The darkness of the room hid the shadows in the corners. Every creak of metal was the scrape of bone on steel.

Steady footsteps thumped by overhead as the watch stood guard on the scaffolding. Whispered comments and a muffled laugh carried on the still, hot air. Summer had come early to the East Bay. Michelle kicked the tangled sheet away from her legs and swatted at a buzzing mosquito.

"Great," she mumbled. "I'll die of West Nile virus instead of the Z virus." A slap killed the bug against her arm. She wiped it away and swiped her hand across her shirt. With a sigh, she turned her back on her bed. She wouldn't be sleeping the rest of the night. Maybe she could trade watch shifts with someone and start her day now.

In minutes, she was dressed and checking the watch schedule on the door of the solar battery room. She trotted over to Jim Evans' trailer and caught the man before he finished coming down his stairs. He patted her on the shoulder and smiled as he turned back to get a few more hours of sleep before the next watch change.

"I'll be taking Jim's place tonight," she informed Ran and Cody once she climbed the stairs. They nodded and headed off to their trailer and sleep as Edward Gonsalves showed up and took a spot at the wall as well.

"Do you want us to say hi to Teddy for you?" Ran added over her shoulder as they started down the stairs.

"No, that's okay. Don't bother him," she said, wishing her tears weren't so close to falling.

The girl ran down the rest of the stairs and caught up to her boyfriend. Even as they moved away, Michelle still caught Miranda's words.

"Some people make it so hard."

She turned away and walked to the wall. Her gaze swept the field and beyond. A full Moon gilded the trees and bushes with a silver edge. A stark reminder that the Moon and the Earth didn't care what happened to the puny humans depending on them for everything. The sun came up; the sun went down, day after day, no matter what they all did. A moan wafted over the still air. No matter if they were living or undead.

Raising the rifle to her shoulder, she scanned the area with the night-vision scope. The full Moon blazed enough light for day, albeit in a greenish tint. *Was she making it hard? For herself and Teddy? Was it too much to ask for some stability in this crazy world? She just wanted to feel safe. For people to be reliable, dependable, and stable. To not be constantly reminded they could go off to work and not come back alive.*

She swung her weapon to the south and eyed the skinbags standing and swaying by the red line on the road. Why didn't they all just fall apart? She didn't know how long it took to decompose in a grave, but it had been over a year and still the undead walked and moved across the Earth. The latest news broadcast on the radio said they'd made some headway and reclaimed part of the capital, but Sacramento might as well be the Moon anymore. It wasn't an hour and a half ride in a car anymore and probably wouldn't be again for years. Travel would be like pioneers on the Oregon Trail, not knowing if everyone would survive the trip west.

The hours of her watch duty passed as she covered her area and then traded places with the men on the south wall. A twinge of guilt fluttered through her at the thought of Lila and her daughter at the mercy of the church and Bennett, but she couldn't find an ounce of regret for the absence of Juan Morales. The man had no friends of those who remained at the RV yard. The watch was peaceful and uneventful without the drama the man had seemed to cause wherever he was.

She was back at her favorite section of south-east wall as the sun began to tint the sky a pale pink and the nighttime shadows died. The camp stirred and sounds carried as people came out of trailers and motor homes to start their day. The boys of Rogue Vantage whistled and waved at her and she turned to face them.

"I'll see you at breakfast," she yelled down. "Make sure you wash up first."

"Oh, Mom," echoed from four different voices.

A scream pierced the peaceful morning. She whipped around. A woman stood by the well with the cover off. A bucket lay in a bloody puddle by her feet, and her hands covered her mouth as she tried and failed to not vomit. As the woman, she thought her name was Maggie, turned to the side; Michelle sighted her rifle on the bucket. Her stomach heaved as she saw what had to be an arm and a hand lying in the puddle. A zomb' had fallen in their only source of water.

Straddling the wall, she turned back to yell again to the boys. "Get Jack and Paul. A skinbag is in the well."

She gripped the rifle and jumped down to the dusty field, landing in a cloud of dirt. In a few long strides she was at Maggie's side. "Are you okay?"

Michelle spun, but no one and nothing was in the field with them. She put the strap on her shoulder and gave the woman a hand. The padlock sat on the dry grass and the lid was half on the opening.

"Did you unlock it this morning?"

"No," Maggie mumbled, shaking her head. "The lock was broke and on the ground. I thought someone did it last night and didn't have time to replace it yet."

Michelle sidled past the bloody body part and kicked the cover aside. Leaning over, she gazed down into the well. What was in there was so twisted she couldn't tell if it were parts or a whole body.

"What are we going to do?" Maggie cried, wringing her hands together.

"I don't know," Michelle said. She leaned down and picked up the padlock. The hasp had been cut with bolt cutters. This wasn't an accident, with someone forgetting to put the lock back on and a zomb' stumbling in. This was deliberate.

She squeezed the metal in her hand until the sharp edge cut into her palm. Didn't take much thinking to know exactly who had done it. A mile or so south sat the Fruitful Harvest Church and its twisted followers, along with a very pissed off Reverend Bennett.

* * *

Commander Canida stepped to the fire and raised his hand. Silence fell over the group as Teddy leaned against a post and crossed his arms on his chest. As far as he was concerned, all the talking had accomplished nothing today.

Talked through breakfast.

Talked through lunch.

They would have talked through dinner but Suz and Dr. Shannon called for silence for the meal. He didn't need any more talking to know what he needed to know. They had an enemy. Point him in the right direction and say 'go.' Talking didn't accomplish anything, pre-Z or not.

"People," Jack said, his voice tired and raw. "We can't go off half-cocked. Even if the people of the church sabotaged the well, that is not our primary concern."

A roar built from the crowd, cutting the man off half-sentence. Pockets of two, three, or four people gathered, carrying on their own, private conversations. He listened with half an ear as the commander continued once silence resumed.

"We have no permanent source of water. Whatever drill rig they used before we came is no longer here and the RVers—sorry, Rogue Vantage, don't know what happened to it. We have enough manpower to dig a well, but not the time with summer just weeks away, if not sooner. Maybe if the governor or the government pulls itself together we might be able to get things like wells and trading posts, but I'm not holding my breath. The army left us to deal with the ZA at The Streets of Brentwood and more than a year later and we are still on our own."

Cheers went up and filled the campfire circle. Then Maggie, the woman at the well this morning stepped forward into the firelight. She held her hand out, the padlock sitting in her palm.

"We'll make do, because we always have. But, what are you going to do about this?" She shook her hand. "What about the assholes who did this?"

"Maggie, we don't know for sure it was Bennett's people."

She laughed and sneered at him. "Right. Like some random renegades we haven't met yet came by and broke the lock and threw that ... that thing down there and left. I've been to that church—once. He spews nothing but evil. He thinks we are sinners here with unwed pairings and unorthodox couples. Well I say to hell with him and his followers. We are doing fine here and we own this place and I'm not letting him drive me away."

Opening her hand, she dropped the padlock at Jack's feet, the sound of metal against pavement carrying in the sudden silence.

Teddy stood back as the camp divided itself between Jack and Paul on one side and Maggie and a group of the younger members of their compound. When they started glaring at each other, he stepped forward.

"Now, I haven't been here from the start, back at the shopping mall, but when I came here with Seth, Ran, and Cody from Pittsburg, you all welcomed me, like a family. I've seen you all have each other's backs, pull together. I've seen you divvy out the chores so no one group is overworked or lazing around doing nothing. Everyone does his or her share."

He winked at Dylan. "Even the Rogue Vantage pulls their weight. But, Jack has the biggest load, and from what I've seen you've been confident in him from the beginning to be the voice of reason in a crazy world. If the commander says we have to be sure before we go vigilante, I have to stand with him, like it or not."

Seth and Emily, Cody and Ran stood by his side. Jed and Beth took a few steps toward him and others filled in the space until Maggie and a few others were left standing alone. The woman whispered to her group and they turned to look at Jack as she spoke.

"Well, since it is more important to get water than to start a war, we've willing to wait to see what happens." She pointed her finger at the commander. "But we won't wait forever."

Taking a deep breath as Maggie's group faded into the darkness, Teddy started when a hand grasped his. He looked down to see Dylan staring up at him.

"Man, that was bitchin,' dude."

Teddy started laughing. "You have been spending way too much time with Cody."

"And you've been spending no time with Mom."

He squatted down in front of the little boy. "We'll figure it out; you don't need to worry about grown-up problems."

Dylan put his hands on Teddy's shoulders like they were talking man-to-man. He felt his heart squeeze with the unfairness of this world on children. Sooner, rather than later, the boys would be called on to hunt for the undead and chase down renegades. They would have to grow up before their time. Hell, they already were.

"She has nightmares, you know. They were doing better, but they came back. She used to call out for Mitch, her husband, you know. But now she says your name too."

Teddy looked into bright brown eyes and sighed, his heart aching. "I'm sorry about that, Dylan. Really I am. But I don't know what I can do about it unless she lets me know we're okay. She has to make the next move."

"Well," Dylan said, his head tilted to the side. "You could sleep with her. Then she wouldn't have to yell for you."

He hadn't blushed so hard in years. Heat filled his face and he looked right and left to make sure no one overheard. He just shook his head at the boy. He'd like nothing better than Michelle in his bed, but tonight when everyone had moved to the area between him and Jack, she'd stood ten feet away and never looked his way, even when she left.

CHAPTER SEVENTEEN

Rule #10   *Anger in the zombie apocalypse is a waste of energy. The undead don't care if you are mad, sad, or glad. Save your energy for what is important . . . survival.*

Michelle looked up from scrubbing clothes to see Teddy and the group leaving for zombie hunting duty for the day. As the man turned, she ducked her head to stare at gray, sudsy, wash water. By the time she brought her head back up, the gate was clanging shut.

His loud laughter carried on the still morning air before the roar of car engines drowned it out. With burning rubber, the cars and men were gone for the day again. *As if they were a bunch of teenagers living in a video game come to life.*

"That anger keeping you comfy at night?" Emily asked as she waddled up beside her and started sorting clothes into piles.

"I'm fine," she gritted out through her clenched teeth. "A woman doesn't have to have a man to survive, even in the apocalypse."

"It's not what you have to have, it's what you want." Emily stared at her. "What do you want, Michelle?"

She grabbed a wad of wet cloth and rubbed it against the washboard, thankful it was durable denim. What did she want? She used to know.

Safety.

Security.

Dependability.

All of that was ripped away in a day.

She'd thought she got it back when they'd arrived at The Streets of Brentwood, with its strong buildings, only to have a madman steal it in a day full of zombie suicide bombers.

She'd been happy here in the RV yard with her daily chores and the boys of Rogue Vantage and then Teddy. But something always seemed to chip away at the foundation of her security.

Bennett.

The undead.

Teddy and his zest for riding out to danger like a hot-dogging cop.

Even the man's stupid inability to see she had risked it all for him.

"I just want to be safe," she whispered.

Emily wrapped an arm around her shoulders. "When were you ever safe?"

Her head came up with a start. "I was safe before all this." She flung her arms around as if to encompass the whole zombie apocalypse.

"Were you?" her friend asked. "You lived in San Francisco. Not exactly the safest city in the world. Your husband was a cop, risking his life every day. Safety is an illusion. One we give ourselves to get through the day. We're no more in danger today than any other day on this planet. Only the things putting us in danger have changed. I was part of the high-and-mighty one percent. Let me tell you, going out into the world was to see how easily the French Revolution happened. The haves and the have nots have always done battle. Just that these days it is for food and water. There is no safety. There never was. Just a thin civilized veneer that was all too easy to rip away. If we'd had true safety, it wouldn't have fallen so fast.

"Do you remember the Internet? That stupid hash tag #firstworldproblems? What I wouldn't give for some of them now. Long lines at the post office. The wrong drink at Starbuck's. The dry cleaning not ready. The ZA is the great equalizer. There is no more First World. We all get to be Third World countries now."

Michelle flung the clothing into the water. "This sucks."

Emily squeezed her shoulders and hugged her. "Yes it does. But having someone at your side can make it suck a little less."

"The man could at least acknowledge I went out the gate to save his sorry ass."

With a laugh, Emily used a T-shirt to sop up the spilled water and pulled the pile closer to the washtub. "How long were you married?"

"Seven years. Why?"

"Over the years, men learn what to say and do and what not to say and do. At least if they're smart, they do. Teddy never married and you two hardly know each other. It takes time to get the nuances right."

She sighed. "You think I'm being foolish, don't you. Making something out of nothing."

Emily held her hands up in the air. "Hey, don't look at me. I'm the Queen of something out of nothing. I can get angry or sad at the drop of a hat."

Laughing, she started scrubbing clothes again. "I don't know how you make me laugh when I want to cry; between Teddy and worrying about the boys and the fact that this is the last of the semi-treated water for cleaning I should be balled up in a corner somewhere crying my eyes out."

"I've told you. No crying in the zombie apocalypse." Emily shook her finger in her face.

"Yes, mother."

"I am not old enough to be your mother."

"But you are going to be a mom."

Emily looked down at her now enormous stomach and gently rubbed it in a circle. A glow radiated from her face. Michelle caught her breath.

"Some things are much more important than misunderstandings."

"Yes, there are." She stared to the gate and beyond it to the now-empty road.

* * *

In the dull heat of afternoon, the scavenger group came back with a truckload of bottled water. Although a welcome sight, it wasn't nearly enough for all the needs of the group and Jack made it clear as soon as it was off-loaded that the water would be used for cooking first. Mumbling filtered over the group.

"Anyone who doesn't like it knows where the gate is. Nothing is keeping you here. Anyone can leave at any time they want," the commander said.

No one moved an inch.

"We share in the good times and in the bad. Right now is a bad patch, but we will get through this."

People nodded and started walking away. A commotion built at the gate. Tires squealed against the asphalt and someone laid on the vehicle's horn nonstop. Michelle turned and spotted the hunting party at the gate. She set off in a run, her heart thumping in time with her pounding feet. She slid to a stop at the metal barrier.

Her heart was in her throat as four men lifted a fifth from the back of the truck. Teddy's limp body hung between them. She bit her lip to stop the scream rising. A groan issued from his lips and Michelle heaved a giant sigh of relief.

Her foot tapped on the ground as the gate stayed closed. Turning, she saw Jack at the controls, his hand over Cody's. The young man argued with the commander, but the words were muffled in her head beneath the roar of the blood zooming through her body.

"Open the gate, Jack," Josh Logan yelled from the other side.

Canida strode to the gate. "Not until I know it's safe for the compound. The man is covered in blood. His or something else's?"

Her head whipped around. Teddy's jeans were dark indigo with blood soaking through the fabric, glistening in the sunlight. A belt was wrapped around his thigh in a makeshift tourniquet. Hands fisted at her sides as the past and present collided in her brain, and all she wanted to do was rip the gate open.

Josh stepped up to the metal barrier. "He's been shot. No bites. No contamination."

Shot? Who would shoot Teddy? The men in the group were his friends. They always had each other's back.

The welcome sound of the gate opening filled her ears as Jack gave the signal to Cody and moved to the side. Teddy's ebony face held a gray tinge as the men hustled by and headed for Dr. Shannon's trailer, now an infirmary.

She paced back and forth on the asphalt while the men carried him in and filed out down the stairs. Catching the swinging door, she catapulted into the makeshift hospital. She slid to a stop at the doorway to the bedroom. Shannon was already cutting Teddy's jeans and ripping them up to his thigh. The doctor's hands slid over the bloody flesh, poking and prodding.

Shannon looked up at Michelle. "You might not want to be here."

She started to argue when a small childish voice cried out, "Not Mr. Teddy."

Michelle squatted down and gathered Dylan into her arms. "Sweetie, you need to leave. You shouldn't be here. I'll stay and watch over Teddy. I promise he'll be fine."

One small eyebrow arched over his wet eyes. "Like you can promise that. This is the ZA."

Left speechless, Michelle stepped back as Shannon turned to the little boy. "Can you go get Ran? I've been teaching her some doctoring and I need her help."

"Yes, Dr. Shannon," he yelled as he ran out the door, slamming it as he went.

"Thanks for the quick thinking. I was at a loss."

"Well, I do need her help. She managed to save Seth by cutting and cauterizing his bite wounds. I'm praying we can do the same for Mr. Ridgewood. His pants are covered in blood and guts that I'm pretty sure aren't his own."

Michelle leaned in closer and spotted the pieces of flesh she'd assumed were Teddy's. The black threads running through pale flesh should have alerted her they were not. Her throat went dry and her mind tumbled to a dozen dark places.

"What about the bullet?" she whispered, envisioning digging into his leg to get it out with primitive tools and hardly any drugs to dull the pain.

"I checked. It's a through and through. We at least have that going for us," Shannon said, placing a hand on her shoulder. "If it had nicked an artery, he'd already be dead."

She jumped when the door was yanked open again and Ran vaulted into the trailer. "Dylan said you needed me?" The young woman's eyes caught the sight of Teddy in the bed.

"What do you want me to do?"

Shannon started handing out orders and Ran and Michelle jumped to comply. In short order they had Teddy tied down, a large quantity of alcohol to flush his wound, and pieces of metal heating on the stove top.

"Michelle, I want you by the head of the bed. You need to check his eyes from time to time. If you note any black lines or the opaqueness they get, we'll have to do what needs to be done. Do you understand?"

She swallowed hard against the knot in her throat. "Yes." Grabbing a stool, she took her position by Teddy's face. Sweat poured down his face and pooled on his neck.

Shannon grabbed what looked like a giant syringe and pulled liquid from a jug. Michelle recognized it as the homemade alcohol the men had been brewing. Too strong for consumption they'd been using it to treat injuries for months.

The doctor squirted it into the wound. The bed creaked as the large man thrashed about, only the ropes holding him down on the mattress. A scream built in his throat and erupted from him with a roar. Michelle put a hand on his sweaty face and pried open an eyelid. His gaze was unseeing but his deep brown eyes were as clear as ever.

Shannon put down the syringe and loosened the belt on his thigh. The wound seeped but didn't bubble or flood with blood.

"That's good, right?" she asked.

The doctor nodded. "So far, so good."

Shannon turned to Ran. "I want to cut some of the damaged area away, so have the metal ready. When I go to use them, I want one at a time. When I give you one, take it back to the fire and bring another one, as fast as possible. I don't need you hurt either. So, fast, not sloppy. Understand?"

Ran nodded and stood ready.

Shannon took up a scalpel and Michelle looked away. She concentrated on Teddy's face and Teddy's breathing. She had a job. She could do it.

His back arched and his screams filled the confined space. She tried to rub his face and check his eyes, but she was helpless to do anything for the pain he was in. She would have taken it herself if she could have.

CHAPTER EIGHTEEN

Rule #11   *Karma is a bitch. Don't tempt her. Don't tease her. She will hit you upside the head every time.*

The stench of burning flesh would never leave her lungs. Teddy's bellows had petered out to whimpers and then silence as he passed out. At least, she prayed he'd passed out. His body lay limp and unmoving on the mattress as Ran continued to bring the metal strips and Shannon continued to cauterize the wounds, with a hiss of burning skin and a moan from the man on the bed.

"Check him," Shannon ordered.

With a shaking hand, Michelle lifted his eyelids and gazed at his deep, dark eyes. No lines.

No milky film. She looked up at the doctor and shook her head. The woman nodded and went back to work.

Teddy mumbled as they untied him, turned him over, and branded the exit wound on his thigh. The man was past any movement. Michelle ran a hand over his scalp and wiped away the clammy sweat on his skin.

His body began to shake with tremors.

"He's going into convulsions," Shannon yelled. "Get him on his side. Michelle, keep away from his teeth. Don't let him bite you."

"He's not turning, damn it," she cried back. She grunted as they got him on his side. His eyes flew open and his mouth moved but no sound emerged.

Tears flowed down her face and dampened her shirt as Teddy's shakes slowed and stopped. Her heart raced with dread. She stared at his chest for seconds that seemed like minutes or hours until she could see the shallow ins and outs of his breathing.

"Get the cushions from the couch. We'll keep him on his side so I can check the wounds tonight," Shannon ordered.

Ran left to get the cushions and Michelle stared at Shannon. "I'm not going anywhere."

The woman pulled her long hair back in order and put it into a ponytail. "I'd enjoy the company. I'm afraid it's going to be a long night." She yawned. "I haven't been this tired since my residency."

Michelle fell back onto the stool. "I'm sorry. You can order me out of here if you want to. I don't know what I was thinking, telling you what to do in your space."

Shannon sat on the edge of the bed and grabbed her hand between her own. "You were thinking that you almost lost the man you love. That you still could."

Her mouth gaped open and she slammed it shut. "I—We—There's been no talk of love."

"I've seen you two together. I know love when I see it."

"But all we do is fight and argue, and he has no respect for me. That isn't love. I loved my husband. He was sweet and kind and gentle."

Shannon laughed. "Love is whatever you decide it is. Every couple has its own way of expressing themselves. I would see couples fighting and arguing in my ER all the time. But by the time they were done being treated they were there for each other. Their fear was making them say things they wouldn't have said if they'd been calmer. Blaming each other for the son getting hurt on his bike. Accusing each other of not watching the little girl who fell and got a concussion. And I'm sure whatever you think Teddy did was fear getting in the way too."

"But he . . ."

"No, don't tell me. That's between you two. Life is precious, now more than ever," Shannon said, pointing at Teddy's injuries. "Too precious to waste on misunderstandings and things that could be solved with a plain old discussion."

Michelle looked at the doctor. "You aren't old enough to be such a wise woman."

Shannon stood, stretched, and grimaced as her back cracked. "Medicine makes you old before your time."

She put a hand on Michelle's shoulder. "I'm going to get cleaned up. Just check his eyes from time to time, make sure he isn't burning up, and I'll be right back."

The clang of metal dropping into the sink sent shudders up her spine. The burnt flesh smell lingered in the closed room. Michelle moved around, opening windows and closing the curtains to keep the sun out.

Ran came in with a basin of water and some rags. "Shannon said to give you this." The young girl set it on the dresser and left again.

She took a rag and dipped it into the cool, clear water. The doctor's patients must be higher on the list of needs, along with cooking to get the good stuff, not the cloudy with bleach the rest of them were using. Wringing out the towel, she slowly swiped it across Teddy's head and sweaty face. He moaned in his sleep and Michelle dropped the rag onto the bed in a panic.

A quick look at his eyes proved her panic as unnecessary. His soaked T-shirt clung to his chest and abdomen. She needed help to get his jeans off, but she could do something about the filthy shirt.

Grabbing the scissors Shannon had left on the dresser, she cut the gray shirt off Teddy's body. It came off in pieces as she cut along his arms and by his neck. The shreds of gray material floated to the carpet. She dipped the rag into the water again, wrung it out, and swept the towel across his chest and abdomen. His ebony skin glistened with wetness. Her mouth grew dry. He was so beautiful, even if men hated the idea of being called beautiful. She could think it in her mind. He was like a priceless sculpture in a museum. Her mind floated to their love-making. He was also very much a man of flesh and blood.

When he shivered slightly, Michelle put the towel back in the water and got a sheet to pull over him. His face calmed and he sighed. She placed her hand on his face and leaned in.

"I'm so sorry you got hurt. I would take it away if I could."

* * *

Voices. Voices came from the other side of the house.

A woman's cry. A man's angry baritone.

The sound of flesh hitting flesh.

Teddy wallowed in a deep fog. His thoughts scrambled between here and there, now and before. Flashes of light pierced his eyeballs and cleaved his head in two. Pain shot through his legs and slammed into his stomach.

Something cool covered his face. A calm voice led him out of the darkness. His eyelids were heavy. Heavier than lifting a dead body into a pile. Finally, they pried open and Michelle's face came into view. His breath came rough and hard from his throat as if he'd run miles to escape the undead.

"Teddy," she whispered with a smile on her face.

"Michelle." His voice cracked and his throat ached.

"Don't move. You were hurt." She put her hand on his shoulder to hold him down.

As if that small hand could keep him in place, he struggled to sit up. His body refused to obey his command. Hurt? He couldn't remember being hurt.

A bottle of water appeared in front of his eyes. Michelle held his head up and helped him drink a few sips. He would have guzzled the whole thing but she pulled it away.

"Dr. Shannon said just a few sips until we see if you keep it down."

He struggled to remember why he would need to see Dr. Shannon and be in bed. Vague wisps of sights and sounds filtered through the fog in his brain.

Voices.

Crying and yelling.

The sound of a slap, echoing in the still air.

The explosion of a gunshot.

Agony and pain.

"Teddy," she said, wiping the cool rag over his face and head. "Do you remember what happened? The men said they didn't see anything but you on the ground by a skinbag, with a gunshot wound in your leg."

"It's all fuzzy. Like I almost do know, but I don't."

"It's okay. Once you've rested, I'm sure you'll remember."

He didn't have Michelle's confidence. In the back of his mind laid a worm of thought, telling him he had to remember. That it was very important.

He shook his head. Maybe if he put his mind elsewhere, it would come to him. Not as if he didn't have enough going on to think about. Like the pain in his leg, the scent of burned flesh in the room, and Michelle at his side, taking care of him. The last thought was the most pleasant one to keep his mind on.

"You're here. With me."

She put a damp hand on his face and stared into his eyes. "Where else would I be?"

He smiled. "Well, lately it's been anywhere but where I am."

Her smile fell. "I'm so sorry, Teddy. I've been acting like a teenage girl having a hissy fit. Something I've had several people nice enough to point out."

Not missing the sarcasm in her voice, Teddy laughed slightly. "Well, you have the body of a teenage girl, so why not the attitude too?"

"Teddy Ridgewood, don't make me angry with you again." Her voice dwindled to nothing and tears filled her eyes before running down her dusty face.

He refused to look down his body and it hurt to look at her face with the tears filling those beautiful eyes. Grabbing her hand, he closed his eyes.

"Tell me the truth now. Did the doctor have to take my leg? Is that why everything hurts? Why I can't move? Why you're crying all over me?"

Her breath caught on a hiccup and hitched. "Teddy, open your eyes. Your leg is fine and attached. Well, mostly okay. She did have to cut some around the wound and we had to burn it some to protect you, the same as Miranda did for Seth and his hand."

He swallowed the knot in his throat and his gaze followed her hand to where it rested on his bare leg. The flesh was red and ugly, but his leg was still there. He took a deep breath and wiggled his toes and moved his foot. The pain had him gulping in air and cursing under his breath, but it was worth it to see his leg there and in working order.

A knock came at the door and it opened with Shannon sticking her head inside. "How's the patient doing?"

Michelle jumped up from her seat. "He's awake and moving his toes."

The doctor stepped into the room and Michelle moved back against the door. Shannon pressed and prodded with more cursing from Teddy, but his eyes stayed on Michelle the whole time.

"I'm going to give you some sleeping pills."

Teddy started to grumble, but the doctor held her hand up.

"No arguing with me. It is going to get worse before it gets better. But there is no leakage and best of all, no black lines."

He stared at his leg. "Not to piss off Karma or the fates or whoever, but, would you be able to see black lines on my skin?"

Michelle laughed and Shannon joined in. "I've seen enough dark-skinned and African-American undead to recognize the signs," the doctor said. "Actually, with your skin tone I would expect the lines to be lighter, maybe even a beige color. I saw some in the hospital that were blood red against black skin."

She handed the pills in a blister pack to Michelle. "Make sure he takes these. Once he falls asleep, I'll take over."

"But I want to stay."

"No arguing from you either. You've been here all day with no food and no breaks. Your boys have been asking for you. Get some food. Get some sleep. I'm sure Teddy will be fighting me to get up and out of this bed by tomorrow."

"Fine," Michelle mumbled.

Shannon laughed as she left the room and shut the door behind her.

Michelle handed the pills to Teddy and got the bottle of water. With some fumbling of getting the medication and water into him, they managed to spill on the bed, but finally the pills were down and going to work.

"I'm sorry," they intoned in unison.

"I'm sorry I treated you like you had no brain. I'm glad my momma can't see me now. She always told me a woman was your better half. She would be there to have your back and to be by your side. The best ones would die for you and you'd be willing to die for them."

She jumped up from the bed and started pacing the floor. Teddy lay silent as tears flooded those beautiful dark eyes. Pain radiated from them as her gaze hit him.

"I love you, Michelle."

Stopping mid step, her face paled to white and her eyes widened. "I can't do this. I thought I could, but I can't. I was a cop's wife and I can't be a zombie hunter's mistress or girlfriend or whatever this is. I can't sit here day after day and wonder if you'll come home hurt or not come home at all. Been there, done that. I can't do it anymore."

He raised himself up on his elbow and met her eyes. "Come out there with me."

Her fist came to her chest as if her heart was going to burst out of it. "I can't do that. I can't."

She turned and yanked the door open and ran out. The outer door slammed shut before he could call her back.

CHAPTER NINETEEN

Rule #12   *Don't ask anyone to do something you aren't willing to do yourself. In other words, grow a pair. If there was ever a time to pull up the big girl panties, the zombie apocalypse would be it.*

Michelle sat alone in her motor home, rocking in a chair, staring at the gold shag carpet. The day gave way to twilight and still she sat in the dark, thankfully no longer able to see the old, matted carpet. Her mind swirled in a million directions at once. Images of Mitch coming up their sidewalk bombarded her. They superimposed themselves on Teddy being carried to the makeshift hospital.

She cried. She laughed and stopped herself when it rang out in hysterics. She wanted to go to sleep and hide from the world. She wanted to be brave enough to not hide at all. She'd been hiding for over a year and nothing had changed. The undead still walked the Earth and humans were still an endangered species, at least the living ones. Because there were more than enough of the undead ones.

Pushing against her knees, Michelle got out of the chair like an arthritic old woman. Her stomach growled to remind her she hadn't eaten all day. She stood at the sink and turned the cold water knob. A few drops fell and plunked in the empty sink.

Her head swum. The tanks of the motor home had been full last week. A different fear gnawed at her. Humans needed water. They could go days without food, but they needed water. Clean, potable water. She grabbed the pot on the nearby stove and headed outside. Silence filled the yard as she came down the steps. A small group sat by the fire pit, but the rest of the area was empty of people. Her ears hummed with nothing but the repel sound. Loud and echoing without the hum of people going about life.

She walked up to the group and spotted Seth.

"How's Emily doing?" Her friend was back on bed rest, at the doctor's orders, as her due date approached. As her stomach had expanded, her breathing had become labored and Shannon ordered Emily to stay in bed. Another worry to add to the long list in her head.

Seth looked up. "She's cranky as hell. Staying in bed is not her idea of a fun time."

She laughed. "I can imagine. Her idea of fun is out hunting zombies."

"How's Teddy doing?"

"Shannon says he'll be fine. I'm sure he will be. Nothing fazes the King of Pittsburg." Her voice caught at her undertone of bitter sarcasm.

"That's true," Seth replied, obviously missing her tone altogether.

"Where is everyone?" she said, trying to change the subject to something less volatile than Teddy and their now nonexistent relationship. There weren't many places to go after a man said 'I love you' and you ran away instead of returning the sentiment.

Seth threw a log on the fire and turned to her. "Well, there was an explosion and fire earlier to the north, so Jack and Paul took a group to make sure it was an accident and not a diversion or something."

"You don't think it's an attack, do you?" Her breath caught. Would they never be safe?

"Jack didn't think so. He radioed a while ago to say it looked like a propane tank at the hotel over there. But they are checking the area to be sure."

She sighed. "What about everyone else? They didn't take everyone, did they?"

"No," Seth said, running a hand through his long hair. "A lot of folks are sick."

"Sick," she whispered. "Not from the virus. It can't be. Not again."

He ran a hand over his face. "Shannon isn't sure yet. It came on right after dinner. But Jim is sick, along with Joseph and Robert Jones. She quarantined them to one trailer. Maggie and her friends are sick too. The doctor put them together in another trailer. So far, the kids and the younger people seem okay. Josh and Suz put them in the office building for safety."

He didn't need to say what safety. He meant if the sick ones died and turned, the kids would be behind cement walls. Her head spun. While she'd been having a pity party for one, the camp had fallen apart. Her boys must be going out of their minds. They'd needed her and she'd been so wrapped up in herself she'd ignored her responsibilities.

"I have to check on the kids," she announced.

Seth nodded. "I saw them earlier, but I'm sure the Rogue Vantage would like to see their mom."

She smiled weakly. "I'm sure I'd like to see them too."

Berating herself all the way to the office building, she strode as quickly as possible, her heart racing in time with her steps. Miranda and Cody sat on chairs at the doorway. Ran sat sharpening the large machete she carried everywhere and the young man flipped pages in an old magazine, the pages frayed and falling out. Another casualty of the end of the world as we know it. Michelle sighed, thinking of the last book she'd read, a wonderful, rich and lavish, historical romance by her favorite author. Back before everything went to hell she'd been savoring it, a chapter at a time at bedtime. The book was wasted space in her one allowable duffel bag and probably still lay on her nightstand in the house in San Francisco, with a turned down page to mark where she'd stopped reading the night before she'd left. She shivered at the vision of millions of homes in stasis. A world full of Pompeii circa 79 A D or Roanoke Island 1590, with civilization forever frozen in the Pre-Z virus time.

Shaking her head, she walked up to Cody and Ran. "Came to check on the boys and the other kids too. How is everyone doing?"

Cody closed the magazine, something with surfboards on the cover. "We fed them a while ago, and then Beth was going to do some reading and writing lessons and Jed was going to teach them how to work the ham radio. I think he said something about talking with the capital yesterday and maybe contacting Los Angeles tonight."

"The boys will like that, I'm sure," she murmured, pushing open the door.

The ham radio sat unattended on the desk in the front office, low static filling the room, interrupted by random voices. She gave it a glance and headed to the storeroom in the back. Finding the door locked, she knocked and called out to the kids to let them know it was okay to let her in.

"It's Michelle. I'm not sick. Let me in."

Loud whispering echoed from behind the door. She raised her hand to knock again, but the sound of a lock being turned clinked and the door opened. Bryant's dark face filled the slim opening.

"Don't be mad," he cried, tears running down his face.

She sighed. How many times had she said that to her mom, just before she said something guaranteed to anger the woman? Placing her hand on the wood, she pushed the door open.

Her gaze swept a room that was nowhere crowded enough for how many people should be inside. Not to mention Jed and Beth were nowhere in sight. Bryant and Aiden were the tallest people in the room.

"I'm not mad," she said in the calmest voice she could manage. "Where are Beth and Jed? They're supposed to be babysit—I mean, supervising you."

Aiden stepped up beside his friend. "They went to kill Reverend Bennett."

The blood left her head and pooled in her gut. She was going to vomit. She'd thought—they'd all thought, Beth was over her obsession with the church's teachings. Wait …

"What do you mean, *they* went to kill him? Don't you mean, Beth went and Jed went after her?"

Bryant shook his head. "No, they planned it. Me and Aidan heard them talking."

"Aidan and I," she corrected on autopilot.

"Whatev," he continued. "They weren't crazy-like or anything. Beth said it was the perfect time with most everyone gone and the rest sick and Jed agreed and pointed out that the northeast corner wasn't covered tonight. Not enough people for patrol or something like that."

Her mind splintered with too many thoughts at once. The young man and woman were outside the compound in the dark on a suicide mission. Not enough people to guard the walls. The leaders not available for help. The rest sick in bed. Who did that leave?

Shannon was their only doctor and needed here with the ill.

Teddy was in bed and injured.

Seth had to stay and watch over Emily.

That left Cody, Miranda, and her.

She took a deep breath. That left Cody, Miranda, and her. *Time to shit or get off the pot, girl.* This was the zombie apocalypse and everyone did their part. She'd been coasting for too long, thinking she was contributing by washing clothes and walking patrol on the walls, protected by the constant repel sound. A nice safe princess in a castle.

Her stomach twisted into knots and bile rose in her throat. She'd sat back and let others do what she could have done, if only she'd been brave enough to do it. If she wanted safety and security, she would have to get it for herself.

"Ryde," Bryant said.

"What?" Michelle asked as the boys' conversation finally filtered through her churning thoughts.

"Ryde. R. y. d. e," Bryant repeated. "Commander Jack was talking to Mr. Seth. He said he sent some guys to check it out and they radioed back to Jed that the recon, recon—something or other was good to go. Then Commander Jack told Mr. Seth that if the explosion was a decoy and something happened with the sickies that we were all going to meet in Ryde."

"Where in the hell is Ryde? Is that the name of a town?"

"It's down the river," Miranda piped up from the doorway. "Biggest thing there is a hotel. Population something like two hundred pre-Z. Right on the Sacramento River."

"Dudes, where's Beth and Radio Man?" Cody added.

"They took off to kill Bennett," Michelle said. "We're going after them."

"Yay," Aiden, Bryant, Connor, and Dylan cheered with the five-year-old Madison twins yelling along with them.

She put her hand up and the hubbub died down. "Ran, Cody, and I are going after them. You are all staying here. Aiden can open and shut the gate, and then he's coming right back here. I want you to lock yourselves in. Don't come out for anything."

Her boys surrounded her and hugged her. Their tears wet her shirt and her tears wet her face.

"I'll be back," she intoned in her best imitation of a famous and popular movie.

Their smiles were all the reward she needed for finally pulling up her Big Girl panties and facing the world they now lived in.

She turned to Ran and Cody as she shut the door and slung her arm over Aiden's shoulder. "Okay, five minutes. Get any weapons you want to take. Don't tell anyone. We will get Jed and Beth back or those sick fucks will die. I've had enough of their toxic church"

CHAPTER TWENTY

Rule #13 *Sacrifices are made every day. Simple ones and hard ones. Never more than in the zombie apocalypse. If it's not worth the sacrifice, it's not worth having.*

There was normal dark and then there was a moonless night in the zombie apocalypse. The Milky Way was clearly visible in the night sky and a billion stars shone down on Earth, but their brightness did nothing for navigating the way down a lonely street.

After seeing to the kids, she'd grabbed a knife to add to her belt, a large pistol in a holster, and her small gun to put down her boot. Ran and Cody grabbed theirs as well and met her at the gate.

Aiden opened it and let them through. She took a second to hug him again. "Watch over your brothers. I will be back if I can. I'm sorry I can't promise more than that. If we aren't back in two hours, go to Beth's father and tell him everything."

He'd hugged her tight and rushed to shut the gate and get back to the safety of the office.

The clang of the metal gate was so much louder when you were on the outside of it. She held her breath until her chest ached. Ran and Cody came up to either side of her and she took another breath. She wasn't alone.

In the silence, the sound of their boots on the asphalt carried down the road. Crickets chirped and cats meowed just as they had since the beginning of time. The moans of the undead at the edge of the repel zone had become as commonplace as the other night sounds.

Ran stopped several feet away from the line of skinbags. "I only see four, maybe five. Cody, get the one coming your way from your three. Michelle, you stand back and we'll take care of this."

She locked her jaw. "I'm not going to be babied all the way there. It's going to take all of us to get our people back. I can do this."

As if to prove the point, she pulled her knife out of the sheath, stepped up to the nearest zomb', and pierced it though the temple. The undead didn't hit the ground before she strode up to the next and dispatched it as well.

She stepped back as Ran and Cody did their job and the moans stopped. Holding her breath, she listened to the now truly silent street. Ran touched her arm and whispered. "We have to make sure Beth and Jed aren't here."

"I don't under . . . oh," she whispered as the realization struck her that the couple might have only made it this far and she'd just made them dead dead. Bile rose in her throat as they turned the bodies over and had to lean close in the darkness to see who they were.

Relief filled her as she turned over the last body and it wasn't Jed or Beth. Standing, she turned to Ran. "You've been out here. What next?"

The young woman leaned in close. "Once we go forward, there is no protection from the sound. No talking except as a warning of incoming zombs. Follow my lead. If I say run, run. If I say stop, stop."

She put her hand on Ran's arm and whispered. "I can do that."

Time passed slowly as they made their way down the street. Ran and Cody would disappear from time to time and the only sound was the thud of a body hitting the ground. The first few times her heart stopped. After a while, she continued walking, believing they would be okay and back again.

After what seemed an eternity, they reached the end of the road, and trashcan fires appeared across the way in the church's parking lot. The moans of their caged undead echoed in the air. Michelle's hands fisted at her sides as they peered around the corner of a house.

Voices and laughter came and went as the men moved around the church building on patrol.

She stared at their movements but no pattern displayed itself. The guards seemed to just wander around the blacktop, stopping from time to time to tease the caged zombs or throw some wood on the fire.

She jumped when a woman's cry came from the building, but she couldn't tell if it were Beth or someone else. All too easily, she could picture the wounded and battle-scarred women she'd seen at the church service. Maybe women crying out for help were a nightly event.

"I counted eight men. Maybe nine," Michelle whispered in Ran's ear.

"Ten. One on the roof," she replied. "I don't think we can take on that many. It isn't like the skinbags."

A knot came into her throat. She didn't think she could kill a living human being. Not unless her life was in danger. Or one of her friends. Could she do it then? She wasn't even sure of that.

"We can't stay out here all night," Ran whispered. "Sooner or later one of them will see us or the skinbags will sniff us out. We can't let them get the upper hand."

She bit her lip. The girl was right. They needed a plan. They needed a guinea pig to get into the church and find out if Beth and Jed were there.

"I'll go," she muttered under her breath before she lost her nerve.

"What?" Ran voiced a tad too loud.

"Who's there?" A man called as he ran toward them, his boot heels thumping on the ground and the sound echoing across the night.

She pushed Ran and Cody back to the darkness on the house's porch. "If I'm not back in thirty minutes, get back to the compound. The others should have returned by now."

"I'm not letting you do this," Ran argued.

"I'll be fine." She shuddered from head to toe. "I think Bennett has the hots for me."

"That just makes it worse," Ran grumbled as she faded into the dark.

She limped into the trees as Cody pulled Miranda against him. She stumbled and made as much noise as possible to let the man find her and not her friends.

"Help," she croaked in a weak, hoarse voice. "Help me."

She crashed into the man as they both reached the sidewalk. Grabbing his shirt, she fell, taking him with her.

"Please, help me. I don't want to be out here. I need to see Reverend Bennett."

The man grabbed a handful of her hair and pulled her to her feet. "We'll just see about that. Maybe he'll let us have some fun with you before you're Resurrected. You can't all be pure enough to be wives."

By the time he'd dragged her to the others; it felt like every hair on her head had been pulled out. Like a bullying in the schoolyard, he pushed her into a circle of men, each one grabbing and pulling at her. She cringed as buttons popped off her shirt and the fabric ripped with a loud sound. Her heart pounded and urged her to run, but she forced herself to stay.

"Please," she begged, holding her ripped shirt to her chest. "I need to see Billy Joe. Please. Tell him Michelle is here."

Out of the corner of her eye, she spotted an enormous man leave the group and head to the church door. He opened it, went inside, and slammed it shut. She could only pray he was going to get Bennett.

The men moved closer, pushing her from man to man. She didn't dare pull her knife; they'd stab her to death. Her heart leapt in her chest. Or undead. She could only hope Bennett was coming.

The door reopened and Billy Joe Bennett filled the space. She shivered, not from cold, but from the lust she saw in his ice-cold eyes. He didn't just want sex with her, he wanted her body and soul, and when that wasn't enough, he'd kill her.

He marched over and pushed men aside like they were paper dolls. Reaching her, he stopped as if noticing all at once that her shirt was hanging on by threads, the tank top beneath just as tattered and torn. The look he turned on his men made the one she'd received downright pleasant.

Bennett grabbed her chin and stared into her eyes. "Who did this to you?"

Her gaze shot right and left. No words came to her dry mouth. How could she blame one when they'd all taken part? She just shook her head and stared over his shoulder.

Bennett turned to the big man. "Elias, sort it out. But by morning I want two dead men, one dead wife, and the children banished from the church. Bring the remaining wife to me."

"Yes, Reverend Bennett," Elias replied in a deep baritone.

She shivered. Hades at the gates of Hell couldn't sound more terrifying. The big man was going to do exactly what Billy Joe had ordered, no questions asked. She'd studied cults in college, but she'd never been this close to the drenched evil they spewed. It was surreal to hear a man order others to death and see another man having no problem with doing the deed.

Bennett unbuttoned his shirt, pulled it off, and draped it over her shoulders. The stench of musk and sex clung to the cloth. She wanted nothing more than to rip it off and fling it to the ground, but that wouldn't get her inside safely.

"Thank you," she whispered, trying not to clench her teeth.

"Anything for you, fair Michelle." His hand ran over her tangled hair and down her back.

"Let's go inside," he uttered as he held open the door for her. As it slammed shut and silenced the outside, the sounds from within became clear. Whimpers and cries filtered down the hall. The sound of slapping flesh echoed louder and louder as they reached the church.

Michelle stumbled into hell. She tried to take it in all at once, but her mind refused to process what she was seeing. Medieval torches in wall holders flooded the room with flickering light. They only added to the feel of a torture chamber in a dungeon. The coppery scent of blood filled the room. The sound of leather on naked flesh filled her head.

Please let Ran and Cody get help. I can't do this all alone.

She swayed and a gray mist pulsated from the edge of her vision. Bennett clasped her to his side. She tried to pull away, but the man only held on tighter, his fingers clenched on her shoulder.

"Seems it is a night of visitors from your compound. Young Beth and Jed make an unlikely assassination team, but it appears they did come here to kill me."

He grabbed her by the nape of the neck and turned her to face him. A bloodstained bandage covered his shoulder, with scratches marring the pale skin on his chest.

Her heart thumped in her head. She looked up at him. "I didn't know they were here. I ran away from our camp to get to you. I had no idea anyone else was coming."

His glare softened. She could tell he wanted to believe her; it was evident in his low, relaxed shoulders and the small grin on his face. The grin died as Beth cried out and she flinched.

He whipped her around, her back to his chest, with an out flung arm holding her tight. He leaned down, his hot breath bathing her ear.

"Where's Teddy, your protector?"

"He's back at the compound. I asked him to marry me, but he refused. I knew . . . I mean, I hoped, that you wanted me. I thought I saw something in your eyes when I was here for church. I had a husband once. I want one again. I want a man who is willing to marry me to have me."

"I'll marry you, Michelle. Play your cards right and I might even make you wife number one."

She took a deep breath. He'd believed her. In his lust for her, he'd believe whatever she said. All she had to do was get her friends released and take care of Bennett.

He leaned in closer and nibbled her ear. A shudder ran down her spine. "Just as soon as Jed and Beth die and join the Resurrected.

CHAPTER TWENTY-ONE

This morning
Fruitful Harvest Church

"Let me go. I don't want to go outside," Maya cried, pulling away from him.

Billy Joe tightened his hand on her wrist and slapped her with the other. Her cries died as he yanked her down the aisle of the church and flung open the door. Sunlight flooded his eyes. The moans of the Resurrected sang in his ears.

"Do you hear them, sweet Maya? They know I am anointed as their leader." He pulled her arm and dragged her to the cages. She pushed back and huddled against his chest. Her whimpers and pleas tightened his erection. It ached and pulsated with his heartbeat.

This is what it feels like to be God. To play with human lives like so many toys.

"Come, my angel. We are going on an adventure," he crooned to Maya.

Her feet plodded against the pavement as he dragged her along in his wake. The undead rattled the metal bars and huddled inside their prisons.

"Let me show you that I'm master of this kingdom. Lord of the Resurrected." He pulled her against his raging hard-on. "Master of you."

Tears spilled down her face. Her dark eyes and dark hair made her a younger, weaker version of Michelle Greggs. For now he would be content with the imitation, but one day soon he'd have the real thing. Maya would be until then.

She stumbled as he strode through an open field to a shack beside some railroad tracks. He glanced around; satisfied they were far enough from the church for her screams to go unheeded by the church followers. Not that his men cared what he did with his women, but appearances must be kept up, he confirmed to himself, sweeping his hair back from his face.

He shoved the girl until her back slammed against the wall with a thud. His hand came to her throat and squeezed. Terror widened her eyes and her hands beat against his chest. He leaned in close and inhaled her gasping breaths.

"Say it," he ordered, loosening his grip enough to allow her to talk.

"I'm Michelle. I want you Billy Joe," she muttered between sobs.

His erection turned to stone. He ripped her dress, baring her breasts to his sight. He reached out and grasped one, tightening until the flesh overflowed his hand and Maya screamed. He flipped her around and shoved her back up against the wall. He yanked her dress up and exposed her bare bottom. He'd taken her panties away weeks ago, so he could have her whenever he wanted.

He controlled what she wore.

He controlled what she said.

He controlled whether she lived or died.

Unzipping his pants, he slammed into her. His yells filled the air with the young woman's cries.

"You are mine, Michelle."

"You are mine, Michelle."

"You are always mine."

"You are mine."

A roar sounded from the corner of the shack. Billy Joe yanked back and pulled himself into his pants and zipped them up. He yanked Maya up against him and faced the intruder. Teddy Ridgewood stormed around the building to face him, murder in his eyes. The man's teeth were bared in a growl like a wild animal.

"Mr. Ridgewood, it is poor manners to disrupt a man making love to his wife." He smiled and tried to put any amount of sincerity in his voice he could muster up. To do otherwise was to take the chance he was a dead man.

"That wasn't making love. You were abusing that poor girl. Someone needs to stop you."

Billy Joe grabbed his gun out of the holster and held it to Maya's head. "Gonna stop me? I don't think so. One step closer and Maya dies."

The girl sobbed and tried to hold her torn dress together.

Teddy held his hands up. "Reverend Bennett, it don't have to be like this. Don't hurt her. I'll stay right here and you can go on back home."

Billy Joe almost believed the man, except for his tense body ready to spring and the look in his eyes. The man heard him calling out Michelle's name and he meant to kill Bennett for it.

"I think we'll play this my way, instead," Bennett yelled, moving the gun to Maya's back and shooting her. Before Teddy could move, he had the gun pointed at the big man's chest.

"You killed her," Teddy screamed.

"No I didn't. I've given her resurrection. We just have to wait a little while." The gun in his hand stayed steady as he grasped Maya's long braid and held her up. Her cries weakened as her blood splashed onto the dry, hard ground. A sigh left her body and she went limp, only Billy Joe's hand in her hair holding her up. In less than a moment, her body twitched and her legs jerked and straightened. A moan rose from her throat. Her hands reached out for Ridgewood, the only thing stopping her was Billy Joe's hand in her hair. She moaned and her jaw snapped, her teeth chomping together.

"We're done here," he uttered, pulling the gun again to the Resurrected's back and sending a bullet laced with blood and guts into Teddy's leg.

The big man fell with a groan and his hands grabbed his leg. He let go of the thing that had been Maya and shoved her in Teddy's direction. As she stumbled and fell on him with a loud groan and a grasping of hands, Bennett turned and walked away.

"I'll take care of sweet Michelle for you," he yelled over his shoulder.

* * *

Teddy fought his way out of the nightmare. Again and again he heard Bennett saying Michelle's name. Again and again he stumbled forward to find him hurting the young dark-haired woman. Again and again the bastard shot her and flung the body at him like so much garbage instead of a precious life wasted. His vision blurred with sweat as he struggled to keep the undead girl from biting him. He reached with searching fingers and found his knife. Pulling it, he stabbed it into her temple with a sickening crunch. Hot blood gushed over his chest.

He flung the girl one way and the knife the other. Pushing up from the ground, he searched for Bennett, but double and triple versions of the scenery provided no one around him. He got his leg under him, but it folded and he collapsed to the ground. A groan escaped him.

At the sound of rushing feet, he scrambled to find the knife. He turned to find Josh and Suz running around the edge of the building.

"Teddy," they whispered loudly. "What happened?"

He mumbled a reply of scrambled words and everything went dark.

Opening his eyes, he found it dark still. He rubbed his face. He remembered light and pain and Michelle. His flung-out hand found no one in the darkness. Noises intruded. Yells and moans and cries filled the compound.

"Mr. Teddy," a young voice cried over the pounding of a fist on the metal door of the motor home. "We need you."

"I'm coming," he yelled, pushing up from the bed. Whatever the doctor had given him must have worked. He stood and only swayed slightly. He couldn't put full pressure on his leg, but limping along seemed to work.

He pushed open the door and found the RVers huddled in a group there. Dylan wrapped around Bryant like an extra attached limb.

"What's going on?" he asked, stepping slowly down the stairs.

Six voices, because he noticed Sarah and Stephanie Madison with the boys, all talked at once. He held up a hand. "Aidan, you tell me."

"At dinner, some people said they didn't feel so good. Beth and Jed ran away when they were supposed to watch us like the doctor said. Mom went after them, even though we tried to stop her.

The sick people are skinbags now and attacking people." He took a long breath as he finished his ramble.

His heart sank. He only heard Michelle went after the two runaways until the screams filtered through the fog of his brain. "What sick people? Nobody was sick. Never mind. You kids all get in the trailer here. I'll be back."

Dylan started crying harder. "That's what Mom said too, and she didn't."

He scooted them into the motor home. "One thing at a time. Now, kids."

Teddy shut the door and leaned his back against it. Mayhem ruled the yard. Thrashing bodies and gunshots overloaded his semi-drugged senses. In the middle of the melee he spotted Seth. Rushing over as fast as he could limp, he bowled into several shambling, moaning women and sent them to the ground. Seth turned and handed him a machete.

Once they dispatched the undead near them, they moved to help Shannon and Jim fight off a man trying to drag the doctor to the ground. Teddy waded in, shoving Shannon one way and the skinbag the other. Seth jumped in to put a knife through its skull.

Except for some crying, the yard was silent again.

He turned to Seth. "Where in the hell is Michelle?"

"What do you mean, where is she? She's with the kids, isn't she?"

"The kids came to me. Something about Beth and Jed running away and Michelle going after them."

Jim Evans pushed himself up from the doorway of the trailer, coughing like he was about to hack up a lung. "Where's Beth?"

He shook his head. "I don't know, but I have a real good idea. I'm going to talk to the kids and get the whole story."

By the time he got to the hospital trailer, he just gathered up all the children and brought them back to where the others who were still alive were gathered.

Shannon had gotten a chair and put Jim in it, wrapped in a comforter. Seth had an arm around Joseph Jones' shoulders. The man was bent over, crying, his eyes red-rimmed and blood coating his hands. His husband, Bob was not at his ever-present spot by his side.

The boys grabbed a bench and pulled it over. The kids sat down, oldest to youngest, Dylan huddled with Connor and the Madison twins in a sniveling ball.

Teddy went over and leaned against the trailer with a sigh, his thigh on fire and screaming in pain. "Aidan, start at the beginning."

"Jed and Beth were watching us in the office because everyone got sick and Dr. Shannon said we would be safe in the storeroom. Beth told Jed that now was the perfect time to go after Bennett because no one was guarding the walls. They made us promise to stay in the storeroom, but they went out a back window and over the fence. When Mom came to check on us she made us tell her everything too. She took Ran and Cody and they went after Beth and Jed, but they aren't back yet. Then all the noise and yelling and shooting started and we ran to get Mr. Teddy."

"Why would she go?" Jim muttered. "I thought she was all better."

"She went to kill that sick bastard," Dylan piped up, with all the kids nodding along.

Jim struggled to get up from his chair, falling back and coughing until he was red in the face. "I have to save her."

Shannon put her hands on his chest. "You aren't going anywhere."

The man started crying and Teddy looked away. He was a mess too with the slightest pressure on his leg sending shock waves of pain to his head, but no one was stopping him from going and getting Michelle away from Bennett.

Or die trying.

CHAPTER TWENTY-TWO

Rule #14   *Say what you mean and mean what you say. Your word is the only thing of value you have left in the zombie apocalypse. Unless a lie will save your ass. Then lie your head off.*

Michelle sat on the grimy carpet and shivered as Bennett's fingers trailed along her bare shoulders. She would throw up if her stomach still held anything to lose after the first two times, the last on Billy Joe's leg. That got her a backhanded slap to the face and the tearing off of his shirt and her tank top underneath.

She took a deep breath and held it. Anything she was suffering now was nothing to the pain and degradation Jed and Beth had been through. The young man was tied to a pillar, his back a mess of cuts and blood. He'd stopped screaming forever ago, the only sound the lashing of a belt against his torn skin.

Tears filled her eyes at Beth tied to another pillar, her skin cut in so many places that Michelle wasn't sure the girl still lived. Someone had carved *whore* across her slightly sagging post-pregnancy stomach. Her long brown hair covered her face, but wisps of it blew with each ragged breath.

The coppery stench of spilled blood gagged her as she fought to keep the bile from spewing forth again. A hand dug into her hair and pulled her head back, the wood of Bennett's 'throne' digging into her bare back between her shoulder blades.

"Do you see what we do to the unfaithful? God has put me in charge of spreading His word, of making sure we are true and devoted to the right way of living."

He pulled her head harder, forcing her back to arch and bringing her breasts within reach. He grabbed a nipple with his fingers and twisted. She pressed her lips together but her moan of pain escaped her throat. Her fingers itched to pull the gun from her boot and put one between Billy Joe's cold blue eyes, but the large man whipping Jed stopped her. She'd never get Bennett and his henchman and she wasn't any good to Jed and Beth if she were dead.

His tight hold relaxed, his fingers strumming across her pebbled nipples, hard in spite of herself.

The other hand smoothing her hair and fondling the strands. Her gorge rose. She'd rather he beat her or cut her or torture her, not this pseudo-petting he seemed to think she enjoyed.

"Are you a virgin?" he asked, his silky tone hissing, bringing the serpent in the garden to mind.

"Of course not," she huffed. "I was married before the flu pandemic and the Z virus."

"He isn't here now, though, is he?"

She turned her head to stare at him. "No, he was attacked and turned. I had to shoot him."

"What about now? Have you been faithful to his memory?"

She blushed and looked away. "That is none of your business."

His hand twisted in her hair and he yanked her off the ground and into his lap. He grasped her chin and forced her to look at him. She shuddered at his crazed eyes, his fingers digging into her skin.

"Or have you been a whore like Beth there and spread your legs wide for every man at your camp?"

She swallowed her inhaled breath, choking and coughing. "Beth is not a whore and neither am I. And even if I were, it is no business of yours. My body belongs to me. I'll give it to whomever I wish."

His hand left her face and latched onto her crouch in a painful grip. "You are a woman. You are weak and willful. Your only place is under a man. Your only place is under me."

The laughter came from some hidden place. A reckless side she didn't know she had. "As if I would have you after Mitch. He was a wonderful man. He was kind and sweet and loving. He had more goodness in his toenail than you have in your whole body."

"What about Teddy Ridgewood? Was he kind and sweet and loving too?"

"No," she uttered, and then spit in his face. "He is big and powerful and can fuck all night."

A look of disgust crossed Bennett's face just before he shoved her off his lap and she hit the floor with a thump of her hip.

"I hope you enjoyed his fucking. Unless you have a thing for the undead, as you call them. After I shot him and threw a resurrected woman at him, I'm sure there isn't much left of Mr. Ridgewood."

"You really should learn to shoot better." Teddy isn't dead. He was there when I left."

He stood up and planted his foot on her chest. Her breath caught and stopped, trapped in her lungs. She couldn't breathe as Billy Joe pressed his foot harder and harder against her. She pushed hands against his leg, the edges of her vision turned to gray and the blood left her brain, making her light-headed. Dizziness filled her, silence roared in her ears.

He lifted his foot.

She sucked in a breath.

He stomped on her chest.

Pain surrounded her. A rib cracked. Her screams echoed in the room.

Blackness beckoned and she ran into it. Anything to escape the pain.

* * *

"Damn, damn, damn," he bellowed, kicking Michelle in the side. She rolled over and moaned.

"Elias," he screamed. "Stop whipping that boy, he's got to be dead by now. Go roundup the men. We're attacking the RV yard. Teddy Ridgewood is going to be dead by the end of the night."

The big man dropped the leather belt to the floor and lumbered down the hallway. The sound of a slamming door echoed into the church a moment later. Michelle's mewling cries irked him. Why did women make you hurt them? All they had to do was know their place. You could treat them like queens if they let you.

He flung himself into his chair. Jed's moans and Beth's sobs indicated they weren't as dead as he thought. Leaping out of the chair, he grabbed the belt Elias had dropped and added a few whacks to the boy's lacerated back. The sound of the leather connecting to bloody flesh, the young man's groans of agony, and the power of dispensing deadly punishment was an aphrodisiac. His erection pounded in his pants, the blood pooled in his groin.

He dropped the belt and marched over to Michelle's unconscious body. Undoing her jeans, he ripped them down to her ankles, too inflamed to pull her boots off. He undid his own pants, crouching over her, when the door slammed again and footsteps pounded down the hall.

Elias slid to a stop at the entrance to the church. "Reverend Bennett, the Resurrected are loose. Someone let them out of the cages. They are all over the parking lot and trying to get in the windows and doors."

He stood up and fixed his pants. Whipping around, his face heated, he glared at Elias. "Well, get some men to round them up. You can manage that, can't you?"

"They're gone."

"Who's gone? I thought you said the Resurrected were around the building."

"The men, sir. They're all gone."

He paced back and forth, a step in each direction, with the beat in his head pounding a tempo of pain. "I want their women and children. They will pay the price for their men's mutiny."

"The families are gone too. The only women left are these two," Elias said, his eyes darting to Michelle on the ground and Beth tied to the pillar. "And your wife and mine."

"This is a trap. The RV camp attacked us before we could attack them."

"Are you sure, sir? I didn't see anyone outside. Just the undead wandering around."

"They are the Resurrected, damn it," Bennett yelled. "And they didn't let themselves out of the cages."

CHAPTER TWENTY-THREE

Rule #15   *Protect the woman you love. She is worth dying for ... even to the undeath.*

"I'm going with you," Seth said with a growl.

Teddy put his hand on the man's shoulder. "You are not. You are staying here with Miss Emily and the children. If I don't make it back ... " He swallowed harshly. "Take the kids and go with Jack and the others."

Sweat dripped off his face and ran into his eyes. The effort of dressing had his nerves jangling. He slid a knife into the sheath on his belt and slammed his gun into the holster. Seth handed him a machete.

"Tell Miss Emily I'm coming back here with Michelle, or I'm not coming back at all."

Seth nodded and turned away, his shoulders slumped as he walked to his trailer. With them all talking at once, he was surrounded by the Rogue Vantage. Aiden's eyes were red and wet streaks ran down his cheeks. Bryant took a deep breath and pulled his shoulders back. Connor and Dylan looked up at him with belief shining in their eyes. He wouldn't let them down.

"I'll get your mom back and the others. I promise."

"Don't make promises you can't keep," Bryant said, glaring at him.

He shook his head. "You're right. I won't bullshit you. I could get killed. But that is all that will stop me. You understand? I will die to get your mother back to you. If we don't make it, go with Miss Emily and Seth."

The boys swarmed him in hugs. His eyes watered and he blinked to clear them. Stepping back, he patted each on his back and watched as they turned and walked away. Dylan went last, turning every few steps to stare at him, before Connor took his hand and pulled him to the fire.

"Jack." A woman's scream resounded from the front gate. The hairs on his arms rose at the desperation inherent in the simple word.

By the time he hobbled his way to the entrance, Jack had it open and a petite woman stumbled into the man's arms.

"Lila," Jack whispered. "What happened?"

"He took her," she mumbled through her split lips. "Juan took her."

Now Teddy recognized Mrs. Morales, even with the rags barely covering her bruised and cut body and her chopped off hair.

"Juan took who?" the commander questioned, sprawling on the cement with Lila cradled in his arms.

"He took Selena. He ran away and took her. You have to get her back," she yelled, grabbing handfuls of Jack's shirt.

"Lila, I told you. I'm not the law. He's her father."

"He took her to be his whore."

Jack's face whitened and he squeezed the woman to his chest. "Even so, I can't do anything. It isn't my place. I have to take care of my people here."

"She's your responsibility, Jack. She's your daughter, mine and yours, not Juan's."

Everyone started talking at once, with the commander's the loudest, and Teddy slipped out of the gate.

He eyed the truck as he limped by, but the noise would let Bennett and his men know he was coming. The element of surprise was all he had going for him. A bum leg, a gun, a knife, and a machete didn't count for much, but it would have to do.

Pressing a little harder with each step, he gritted his teeth and walked through the pain until it was a constant condition. One to ignore, like the monotonous hum to repel the skinbags. As he reached the red line on the street, he searched the area but no undead moaned at the barrier tonight. The tumbled dead bodies marked the group's passage earlier. He glanced at each quickly and found none of his friends.

Cody. Ran. Jed. Beth. He pictured each in his mind and said a prayer he would find them all safe and alive.

Michelle. His mind stumbled along with his feet as he recoiled at the thought of her undeath and tripped over a zomb' in the middle of the road. "Good job, Teddy. Get yourself killed before you even get there. Lotta help you'll be."

He pushed the thoughts of his friends out of his mind. His friends and ... and what exactly was Michelle Greggs. Girlfriend was adolescent and not strong enough for what he felt for that woman. Friend didn't begin to cover it. Mate. He liked the sound of that in his mind. She was his mate. His wife, if they survived the night and she'd have him. He wanted to be Michelle's husband very, very much.

Moans from the church parking lot greeted him as he reached the corner and moved to hide behind pine trees and brush on the corner lot. Flickering torches showed the zombie horde stumbling around across the blacktop. The cage doors swung in the breeze and clanged metal against metal. The breeze also carried the stench of rotting flesh. Teddy pressed a hand to his nose and breathed through his mouth. A crunch of twigs had him whipping around to his left and raising the machete for a skull-bashing.

"It's Ran and Cody," a voice whispered in the dark.

He lowered the weapon with a giant gasp of relief and instantly regretted the deep breath as he was bombarded with the stink of zombs. His gaze swept their faces as the young man and woman stepped out of the shadows of the house.

"Where's Michelle?"

Ran and Cody both turned to stare at the church. "She said to leave if she didn't come out but we couldn't do that," Ran whispered. "We got the cages open and let the skinbags out. We thought we could create a diversion or something. But the men just got their families, hopped in their cars and trucks, and high-tailed it out of here. Guess they had enough of the Fruitful Harvest Church," she finished with an ugly sneer on her pretty face.

"Did everyone go?" Teddy felt the blood leave his head at the thought of Michelle kidnapped and gone. It wasn't like there was an Amber Alert or something anymore. If Bennett took her, he'd never find her. Kidnapped people were hard enough to find in the pre-Z time.

"Bennett didn't show and the big guy, Elias, I think is his name, came out, looked around, and went back in," Cody provided. "I counted thirty-five, women included, the day we were here. At least that many left, minus Bennett, the big dude, and their women."

Teddy smiled. "You did good, Cody."

Miranda punched her boyfriend's arm. "Who woulda thunk?"

The young man smiled like he'd run the game-winning touchdown. "Now, what do we do?"

"*We* don't do anything," Teddy said. "I'm going in there and you two are going back to the RV yard."

"Teddy," they both complained. "At least let us help you get in," Miranda added.

He turned and counted at least twenty skinbags milling around the entrance to the church. "Okay, we do this fast. Cut a path to the door, I go in and you two run like the wind back to camp."

The two nodded and he prayed they listened. He needed all his concentration on getting Michelle and the others out alive, he didn't need two more people to worry about. His heart raced and thumped in his chest. He took a few deep breaths, ran/limped as fast as he could, with Ran and Cody on either side of him.

He grunted as he hacked through necks and chopped into skulls. Pulling the blade from the last head, he took a deep breath and whipped around. The area was clear to the door. He shoved the two kids toward the street. "Go; don't stop until you get back."

Staring until they were swallowed by darkness, Teddy slowly opened the door. He stepped through and closed it with a quiet click. With a flick of his wrist, he flung the blood off the machete and raised it at his side.

Voices came from the end of the hallway. Knowing that was where the church was, he stepped in slow, measured strides to the brightness at the end of the carpeted space. He hugged the wall as he reached the light. His gaze swept the room. A man with a bloody back hung from the wall. He swallowed as the figure turned and light shone on his eyeglasses. Jed moaned. A woman's cries had him rushing forward. Light-brown hair shielded her face, but he still recognized Beth tied to another pillar, blood dripping off her naked body. Teddy gazed long enough to note her chest moving with breaths.

Bennett stood over a form on the floor. He saw red as he glimpsed Michelle's half-naked body sprawled on the carpet at Billy Joe's feet. The man smiled as he yanked her up and pulled her in front of him, his hand cupping her breast.

"If it isn't the man himself," Billy Joe drawled. "The great Teddy Ridgewood. The world's greatest lover, or so I'm told." The man squeezed Michelle's breast until she screamed. Her head came up and her eyes widened as she stared over his shoulder.

Teddy turned, raising the machete. Something hit him in the back of the head. Darkness and the rough texture of the carpet greeted him as Michelle's cries reverberated in his head and the room.

CHAPTER TWENTY-FOUR

Rule #16   *Love isn't a requirement in the zombie apocalypse. But without love, what are you surviving for?*

Tears streamed down her face as Elias turned Teddy's limp body over and tied his hands together in front. Then the large man slapped him across the face. Moans rolled from him as Teddy stirred and sat up.

He was still alive. There was still hope.

He opened his eyes and anger filled them as he stared at her in Bennett's lap. A shudder ran through her. She never wanted that hatred directed at her. She struggled to get away, but Billy Joe put the knife to her throat, pressed hard, and she stilled.

Elias dragged Teddy up to his knees and placed a knife at his throat. Bile rose in her throat. They were going to die and she'd never told him of her love for him. Of her respect for him. Of her belief in him. She mouthed the three little magic words to him and smiled as he mouthed them back.

"None of that," Bennett growled, nicking her with the knife. The warm blood trickled down her neck to her bare chest.

Teddy tried to get up, but Elias yanked an arm around his throat and pulled his head back. The point of the knife pushed his chin up.

"Stop, I'll do whatever you want," she cried. "Just don't kill him, please."

Bennett's laugh skated across her nerves like fingernails on a metal door. "I wouldn't kill Mr. Ridgewood. He would become the new beginning of my Resurrected. He would live forever.

"Besides, I knew you would say that. All women are weak. They will use their lustful bodies to get what they want. All women are whores at heart. They think nothing of breaking their marriage vows. They think nothing of whoring themselves for *the church*. They think nothing of everyone knowing what they are doing. They think their sons don't know, but they do."

His spittle hit her bare skin as Billy Joe ranted and raved. The knife on her skin wavered and fell. She pushed away and jumped up. He grabbed her hair and pulled her back before she could get anywhere. Pulling her back against his chest, he moved the knife to her face. She caught her breath and held it. The man had lost it, even more than before. She didn't even know if it were her he was mad at or some other woman or all women.

"Bet you wouldn't want her if her lovely, lying face was all cut up," Bennett shouted across the room.

Teddy pulled his body straight and his warm brown gaze locked onto hers. "I would love Michelle no matter what she looked like on the outside. I know she is even lovelier on the inside."

Billy Joe stood, taking her with him, his hand still locked in her hair, the other gripping the knife at her throat. "Let's put it to the test, shall we? Let's see if true love is really that true."

"I told you I would do anything to save Teddy," she whispered.

"Of that I have no doubt," Bennett hissed against her ear. "Women are weak and use their feminine wiles at the first sign of trouble. But what will Mr. Ridgewood do to save you?"

He turned his head and yelled across the room. "What will you do, Teddy, to save Michelle?"

"I'll do anything to save her," he said, loud and clear. "Kill me, you can do whatever. Just let her go."

"Teddy, do you know what I thought from the minute I laid eyes on you?"

He shook his head.

"I thought what a great breeder you would be. Like a bull in a pasture of cows. I could breed up an army of warriors. God had a plan for me. The start of a kingdom. And now that is all gone because of you. You and your slut.

"But you are going to fix all of that, Teddy Ridgewood. If you want her to live, you are going to give her to me. To make my wife. And once I do, I'm going to take her here, in this holy church and the last thing you see will be your blood pumping out across the floor as I make her my wife; mind, body, and soul."

A buzzing started in her head. The lighting dimmed and her knees shook. Billy Joe yanked her up as her knees tried to fold.

No. No. No. No.

She yelled the words, but only in her head, as her mouth moved and no sound came out.

Bennett pulled back her head and placed the cold steel of the knife on her throat. She gagged as he increased the pressure until she couldn't swallow.

Just do it. Everything would be over so quickly and she could leave this insane world and she wouldn't see Teddy die. She couldn't see another man she loved die.

Teddy. She'd found love twice in this lifetime. Some people never found it once and she'd known two amazing men. Mitch and Teddy. So different from each other, but so alike in some ways too. They'd give their lives for her. She'd always known that about Mitch and now Teddy had proven it as well. Even injured, he'd rushed to save her. She straightened her back and stared at the man she loved. Putting all her love into her thoughts, she prayed he would see it in her eyes. And in her hand. The one she formed into a gun shape like the kids did and pointed it at Teddy.

Sweat gathered in her eyes and rolled down her face before Teddy blinked back at her. Two blinks. A pause. Two more. Do it, she mouthed to him.

"What do you say, Ridgewood?" Bennett pressed the knife to her neck. She flinched, afraid to move, to breathe.

She stared as Teddy swallowed, his Adam's apple bobbing up and down. The man fought to do what must be done, while she could see it went against everything inside him.

"I give Michelle Greggs to you as your bride. I renounce all claim to her," Teddy whispered. In the silent room it carried as loud as a yell.

"Submit to me," he whispered in her ear. "Submit and Ridgewood will die instead of being resurrected. " Her body trembled as the knife moved from her throat to the back of her head. She lowered her head, stared at the dark carpet through a haze of tears, and wished a thousand anguished deaths on Billy Joe Bennett.

"I claim you and mark you as my wife and helpmate," he intoned in a smug voice. "I mark you with shorn hair to show your fidelity and loyalty as a good wife."

The blade sliced through her hair and she was unable to stop the angry tears from flowing down her face. She stared as handfuls of hair pooled at her feet and a breeze wafted across her bare nape. His hands shook as they grazed her neck. Each slice took eons as he dragged the torture out, fondling her hair and rubbing himself against her body.

"It's only hair," she whispered to herself.

At last, he stopped and dropped the knife to the floor with a muted thud. He clamped his hands on her shoulders and pushed her to her knees.

"Go with God and may you find your wife submissive and pure," the large man intoned from where he stood by Teddy.

"Now you are mine and in your rightful place as a woman, at the feet of a man."

Her teeth clenched as she imagined the gloating smile on his face, his cold-blue eyes heated with lust. Then she reached for the gun in her boot. The tiny .380 that her husband had said was useless for anything bigger than a rat.

She'd left the camp with a gun in a holster and a knife in a sheath in plain view and just as she'd imagined, they'd taken them. But in Bennett's greed to get her partially naked, he'd left her jeans and boots on. He would pay for that stupid mistake.

"Now I'll take my wife, Ridgewood, and it'll be the last thing you see," he crowed, grabbing her neck and spinning her around.

Her arm rose with the gun in her hand. She shoved it against Billy Joe's crotch and fired. The sound hummed in her ears as the man fell over, screaming and grabbing himself. His blood shot across the floor and splattered her face.

Michelle spun around to shoot Elias, praying she'd miss Teddy. Her jaw dropped open as Ran and Cody rushed into the room. Ran swung her machete and hit the large man in the neck. Blood sprayed across the young woman as he toppled to the floor, twitched a few times, and went still. He'd be back in a moment, but she'd let them deal with Elias.

She stood up and turned to finish off Bennett. An older woman knelt beside him. She recognized Roberta, his wife. Reaching down, the woman picked up the fallen knife and turned to Michelle.

She kept her hand steady on the gun. "Don't make me shoot you. He isn't worth it."

"No, he isn't," she whispered, as she plunged the knife into his chest. "You are the Resurrected, my darling."

Michelle jumped, her finger tightening on the trigger as Roberta turned the knife on herself and plunged it into her stomach. She rushed forward, but the hazy veil of death was already appearing in the woman's eyes.

"Why?" she asked, her hand grabbing and clasping the older woman's.

"Now he will be all mine again," she whispered and closed her eyes.

Michelle stood, pulled her jeans up, and took stock. Ran and Cody had cut Teddy loose and rushed to check on Jed and Beth. Ran stepped back and shook her head, raising the machete in front of Beth's mutilated body.

"No," Michelle cried out. "We can't do that to our friends. They deserve to go in peace."

She stood by as Ran cut the ropes holding Beth's limp body to the pillar. The young woman laid her friend on the floor and covered her with a blanket. Cody did the same for Jed. Michelle jumped as they twitched beneath the covers. She moved closer and whispered, "I'm sorry." The sound of the gunshot echoed twice in the cavernous space.

She grabbed a torch off the wall. "This place has known evil, but it once knew goodness." She threw the torch to the floor in front of Roberta and Billy Joe and stared as the flames caught on the carpet and the clothing of the dead.

The others rushed around and followed suit. Teddy ripped the isolation curtains from the rear and added them to the growing flames. The rest caught fire quickly and smoke roiled against the ceiling and started filling the space.

The crackle of fire and the groans of the newly turned followed them as they all rushed to the hallway and the door beyond.

They ran outside and Michelle took a deep breath of fresh air as Teddy took off his shirt, wiped her face, and pulled it over her head.

He grasped her close and kissed her lips.

"I love you."

"I love you."

"If you're done with the lovey-dovey stuff, do you think I could go with you guys?" An unknown voice wavered and cracked from the young girl standing by the empty zomb' cages.

CHAPTER TWENTY-FIVE

"We were kidnapped by—by Bennett's men and brought here," the young woman stuttered. "They gave me to Elias. Said we were married."

She stared over Teddy's shoulder, the flash of flames brightening her green eyes. "He is dead, right?"

Wrapping her arms around her body, she fidgeted from foot to foot like a spooked animal. He wanted to pat her on the back and let her know it would be okay but she looked like a piece of glass that would shatter at a man's touch.

Michelle obviously felt no such concern as she rushed forward and enveloped the girl in her arms. Sobs broke and filled the air with devastation and anguish. The girl's shoulders shook with her cries.

Teddy's jaw clenched and his teeth ground together. No human being should know such despair. Marriage was a sacred bond, of love and

understanding. Not abused by psychopaths for sanctioned rape. The heat at his back and the smoke billowing in clouds around them were a vivid reminder that Bennett and his twisted beliefs were done.

But nothing could bring back Jed and Beth. Two young lives lost in an instant. His hands clenched into fists and tears blurred his vision. The thought of telling Jim his young daughter was dead almost sent him to his knees.

"What's your name?" Michelle's hushed voice reached him.

"April. April Reynolds," the girl replied, her voice cracking. "We were in Antioch, trying to get to Sacramento, but our car broke down on the freeway. Bennett and his followers showed up and we thought we were saved. Saved. What a joke. They killed Aunt Mary. Said Terri was a liar and chopped off her head. Bennett took Maya and gave me to that bastard Elias."

Teddy's heart broke at April's bland retelling of her ordeal. The words recited in a monotone, as if the girl were reading a book about someone else's life. If those men weren't dead already, he would have marched back in through the heat and flames to kill them again. He stared down the road. He could only pray the rest of the 'church' would be harmless without the head of the snake leading them.

Michelle's head came up. "Maya," she said, staring at the inferno.

He shook his head. "Bennett killed her when he shot me."

"Everyone else left before we went in," the young couple explained together.

Ran and Cody stepped forward and introduced themselves. Michelle stepped back to Teddy's side, her shudders vibrating through her body. He swept her into his side and wrapped an arm around her shoulders as the kids chattered about the RV yard and the people there.

Teddy swallowed harshly. The RV yard was no longer the safe haven they had built. At the end of the road in front of them they might find it abandoned and desolate. His gaze swept over the woman at his side. Her chopped hair did nothing to diminish her beauty and strength, but her arms wrapped around her torso as if it were cold instead of the muggy, hot night it was, brought his anger forth again.

He yearned to grab her into his arms and carry her to safety, except safety didn't exist anymore. Certainly not back at the compound, probably empty by now. They wouldn't know until they checked it out.

"Okay, guys," he called out. "We aren't out of here yet. Check your weapons and stick together. The living aren't the only things to worry about."

The three young people walked in front of them, their chatter dying away as they left the parking lot and church inferno behind. Michelle strode at his side, her pea-shooter held at her side.

"You know that thing won't kill anything, right?" he whispered.

"It took care of Billy Joe Bennett well enough," she hissed back.

He held out his hand and took the small gun, looking even smaller in his large hand. Putting it into his pocket, he handed his machete to her.

Moans gathered strength on the road ahead. Ran and Cody rushed forward and took out most of them, a few slipping through to be dealt with by Teddy's gun. Looking around to make sure he hadn't missed any, he spotted Michelle decapitating a rotten skinbag on the sidewalk. Its head rolled one way and its body dropped to the ground with a wet splat.

She turned toward him. "This is cool. No wonder Emily likes it so much. You can take out all your anger on these things."

"Not so fast, zombie-hunter woman," Teddy said, shaking his head. "You can never forget these are people. Or, at least, they were. Someone's mother, father, sister, or brother."

"Or husband," she whispered, her face turning white.

He pulled her in close, knowing the kids had the lookout. "Or husband. You did what you had to do. Would he have wanted to stay undead?"

"No," she mumbled against his chest.

"Jed and Beth would thank us if they could. We do this for the families that wouldn't or couldn't do it."

* * *

Michelle brought her head up and gazed at Teddy's serious face. "For the families."

"For the families," he intoned back.

"Let's go home," Michelle said, turning to continue walking. Her heart rate sped up at Teddy's silence. He hadn't seemed excited to get back to the RV yard at all. He was hiding something, but her fear and sadness kept her silent. Whatever it was, they would know soon enough.

They tramped down the road, their boot heels making the only sound in the coming dawn. She gazed at the sky as the sun rose and painted it with a wash of pink and orange. The trees gleamed with sunlight instead of being black blobs in the dark. How could such simple beauty still exist in the evil world she'd seen?

Stopping at the painted red line, she whipped her head back and forth. "Where's the hum?"

The others spun around, weapons raised. No zombs huddled along the repel barrier, although their moans could be heard further down the road from the direction of the camp.

Her heart rose in her throat. Were they all dead? Emily? The boys? Tears blurred her vision until she scrubbed them away with the heel of her hand. Not her boys. Not her friend Emily.

Teddy started jogging to the entrance of the RV yard and the rest of them followed. About a dozen skinbags pressed against the gate, moaning and rattling the barrier with the squeal of metal.

Michelle swung the machete as one zomb' shambled toward April, the only unarmed member of their group. Ran had tried to give her a knife earlier, but the girl informed them she had no idea how to use it.

April jumped back as the first one hit the ground and Michelle was already on the next. A zomb' was headed for Teddy's back, but she took it out with a swipe of its calf. The thing fell at Teddy's feet. He turned and grinned at her.

"Thanks," he yelled.

"No problem," she yelled back.

Ran and Cody finished up the rest and walked up to the gate. With the skinbags now dead dead, silence filled the morning air.

Where was everyone? Had they all died?

Teddy turned to her. "When I left to get you, a bunch of folks had been sick earlier. They turned and we had to put them down."

Her hand flew to her mouth. "Emily? Rogue Vantage?"

Teddy shook his head. "No, Emily and Seth were fine when I left. The boys too. They demanded I go get their mom."

She smiled slightly, still worried about the total silence. "So where is everyone?"

"The group was headed to Ryde," Cody added. "Should we yell, Teddy?"

Ran rolled her eyes at her boyfriend. "No, Doofus, just climb over and open the gate. We can't stand out here all day."

As if to punctuate the problem, a moan rose from the field beside the RV yard walls. She watched with one eye on the young man scaling the fence and one on the area around them.

Cody jumped down on the other side and raced to the controls. In seconds the metal barrier rolled back and they hurried inside. The gate shut with a clang.

She caught her breath. They were safe inside. It didn't bring the rush she'd expected and anticipated. The yard stood dark and silent, not the bustling hive of activity she'd grown used to in the past year. Safety was an illusion, just as Emily had said.

"Hello? Anyone here?" Teddy called out in his deep baritone.

"Over here," came the reply from the firepit, now unlit with a wisp of smoke curling into the morning air.

They strode over and found Seth huddled over Emily, her cries building in intensity until she ended with a scream loud enough to bring every zombie in the area running for mealtime.

Her emotions warred inside her; did she rush to help Emily or find her boys? Emily's groans settled it. She had to help her friend. Teddy would find out about her little ones, she was sure. The big man loved them as much as she did.

Teddy started peppering Seth with questions and the man answered as best he could with her friend trying to crush his hand in hers.

"Everyone left with Paul, Suz, and Josh for the next safe zone. Jack left with Lila. He gave Paul command until he makes it back ... if he makes it back."

He caught Michelle's eyes. "Paul took the boys and the Madison twins with their group. We stayed for you guys. Emily wouldn't hear of leaving without you. I was going to make her leave if you didn't get back today."

She coughed on a held breath she didn't know she was holding and brought her attention to Emily, crying and panting on a cot.

"Where's Doctor Shannon?"

"She had to go with Jim. He isn't doing well and she had to drag him out of here. He wanted to go after Beth, but Shannon stopped him," Emily got out between moans.

"Where are Jed and Beth?" Seth asked, looking around.

Teddy just shook his head.

Michelle stared down into Emily's face. "I did it all for nothing. Jed and Beth are gone. Bennett killed them."

Emily grabbed her hand. "It is never for nothing. Could you have lived with yourself if you hadn't at least tried?"

A scream erupted from her friend as Emily's body bucked on the cot. Tears for the dead would have to come later. Now was for the living.

She wiped the tears from her eyes and squatted at her friend's side. Michelle tried to keep her voice light and cheerful. "You weren't supposed to have the baby yet. I go away for a few hours and look what happens."

Emily reached up and grasped her shorn hair. "Look at you. You'll be a zombie-hunter yet."

Teddy leaned over. "She already is. You should have seen her, Miss Emily. Whacking skinbags right and left. Protecting my ass. I might have to become the zombie-hunter's man."

"I'll settle for being the zombie-hunter's woman who occasionally saves his butt," she whispered, staring into Teddy's eyes.

He leaned in and his mouth swept across hers. "What about the zombie-hunter's wife?"

She kissed him back. "That too." Her voice caught and wavered. "Yes, I'd like that very much, Teddy Ridgewood."

"Yo, lady having baby here," Emily butted in.

They laughed and got down to the business of birthing a baby. Men could joke about killing zombies, but giving birth was tougher than slaying the undead any day.

She'd quickly sent Ran, Cody, and April on chores to gather what she needed to help Emily and what they would need when they left. Looking around between Emily's contractions, she knew for sure that this was no longer home. Glancing over at Teddy talking to Seth, she knew just as sure home was wherever that big, beautiful, wonderful man was.

"Can I fucking push already?" Emily growled at her.

"Let me look," she growled right back at her.

Emily started crying and Michelle started apologizing.

"Just get it out of me," her friend screamed.

Michelle took a peek under the sheet the kids had brought over for Emily. "I see the head."

Seth ran over and took Emily's hand. "You can do this, sweetheart."

"Don't you sweetheart me. That's what caused all this."

Michelle smiled in spite of the situation. Emily had been declared infertile in her old life and she'd been over the Moon to discover she would have a baby after all.

She turned back to the sheet and reached to guide the baby as best she could. She'd taken a class years ago about emergency birthing, but all she really could do was guide the baby and catch it and pray it was enough.

"Hand me a towel," she ordered and found one quickly in hand. As the baby slid out, she grasped it firmly and set it on the towel. Him on the towel, she saw just as she wrapped him up and brought him to Emily's chest.

"You have a son," she declared, her smile wide enough to split her face. Emily's was just as wide and full of wonder.

"I have a baby," she whispered, her fingers touching his cheek.

Tears slid down Michelle's face as she reached to deal with the afterbirth. She wrapped it in another towel. They could cut the cord in a moment; she just wanted to watch Emily and Seth with their miracle. In the normal world, birth was a miracle. In the Z virus world, it was proof that life went on. Human life.

"It hurts," Emily screamed. "What's happening?"

Michelle's heart raced. *Please don't let her be hemorrhaging. I can't lose her too. Please, God.*

Sometimes God heard prayers, she thought as it wasn't a gushing river of blood she saw between Emily's thighs, but another head.

"I hope you have another name picked out," she said, getting another towel from Ran and bringing out another wrapped bundle. "For your daughter."

Seth took the baby and held it by Emily's face. "Twins," he whispered.

Emily turned her face to her daughter. "Carla Beth. You are named for your father's mother and the sweetest girl I've known."

Seth reached and touched his son. "Jed Robert. You are named for two brave men."

She started in her seat. There was only one Robert among their friends. Wincing, she realized in an instant that wasn't true anymore. Wiping her tears with her forearms, she smiled, wanting to believe their friends and loved ones lived on in these little namesakes.

Michelle finished up and gathered the soiled bundles. She stumbled to a water barrel and scrubbed her bloody hands. She ached, but it was a good ache. Out of all of the tragedy of the last couple of days, there had been a miracle. She smiled. Two miracles.

Someone walked up and wrapped big strong arms around her. She leaned back against Teddy's broad chest. This was safety. This was security. The only kind that lasted. The kind that didn't rely on walls and gates.

"We need to wait here a day or two to let Emily rest, but what do you want to do after that? We could stay here, rebuild, or we could join the others in Ryde."

She stared at the gray concrete walls that now seemed more like a prison than a sanctuary. She turned and gazed at a man willing to be right here where he belonged. She smiled at a man who put her needs and safety first.

"Let's go get our boys, my zombie-hunter husband."

The End

Dear Reader,

I hope you enjoyed Michelle and Teddy's story. From the time I 'met' Teddy in *Love in the Time of Zombies* I knew he would be my next hero. Michelle's back story was so sad that I wanted to give her an extra-special happily ever after.

If you haven't already, you can start the Time of Zombies series with *Love in the Time of Zombies.*

A Time to Kill Zombies, Jack and Lila's story, is book 3.

Walk with the dead, Jill James

Jill James didn't start out wanting to be a writer. She was going to be an astronaut, a lawyer, a doctor, or President of the United States. Life happened and she realized she could be all of those things in the pages of the books she wrote.

She lives in Nevada with her husband who is the inspiration behind all her romance novel heroes.

You can reach Jill online.
email: jill@jilljameswrites.com
Facebook: www.facebook.com/Jill.James.author
Twitter: www.twitter.com/jill_james

or drop a note.
Jill James
P.O. Box 61102
Reno, NV 89506